THE COLOR
OF THE
SKY IS THE
SHAPE
OF THE HEART

THE COLOR
OF THE
SKY IS THE
SHAPE
OF THE HEART

CHESIL

Translated by Takami Nieda

Published in the United States by Soho Teen
an imprint of Soho Press, Inc.
227 W 17th Street
New York, NY 10011

Library of Congress Cataloging-in-Publication Data

Names: Chesil, author. | Nieda, Takami, translator.
The color of the sky is the shape of the heart/Chesil ; translated by Takami Nieda.
Other titles: Jini no pazuru. English
First published in Japanese under the title Jini no pazuru.
Identifiers: LCCN 2021049131

ISBN 978-1-64129-229-0
eISBN 978-1-64129-230-6

Subjects: CYAC: Identity—Fiction. | Koreans—Japan—Fiction.
Koreans—United States—Fiction. | LCGFT: Novels.
LCC PZ7.1.C49768 Co 2022 | DDC [Fic]—dc23
LC record available at https://lccn.loc.gov/2021049131

Interior design: Janine Agro

Printed in the United States of America

10 9 8 7 6 5 4 3 2 1

THE COLOR
OF THE
SKY IS THE
SHAPE
OF THE HEART

Not There

That day was no different than any other. High school was as cruel as ever.

In biology the invisible boy in class, John, burst into tears and hid under the lab table again. He fell over on his back and cried like a baby, slapping his hands on the floor. This had happened before. John was known to have tantrums. He was way more sensitive than the average kid. Maybe seeing the anatomical diagram of a rabbit in the textbook had upset him. Maybe it was just that John was the most gentlehearted boy in the world.

High school really was a cruel place. Actually, it wasn't school but the whole world, and like the world, class went on without pause, as if John didn't exist.

He was bawling his lungs out, yet no one seemed to hear him. None of the students at the school were all that studious, but at that moment, their noses were buried in the textbooks, their necks contorted into impossible angles. It was a strange sight, since it was obvious they weren't the least bit interested in reading what was written in those books. *I must've slept funny and this is how*

I woke up, said the expressions on their faces—on every face in the classroom.

Everyone in school knew John was like this, and yet some kids still sat at the same table as him. It was only when John burst out crying that they noticed. *Oh, so there you are.*

They'd been sitting together before class started, but now they acted like he'd teleported out of nowhere or something.

The kids looked at John with disgust, as if he had a highly infectious disease. Their eyes—every one of them—seemed to say, *Touch him, and your finger will swell up and itch and wreck your whole day.* None of the kids bothered to move to another table though. Whether they moved or not, it was all the same anyway. The classroom was already infected.

It was strange. Although there were, at most, twenty kids in the class, sometimes even I didn't notice John was there until he started crying. When he wasn't crying, John was the best in the world—no, in the universe—at making himself disappear. In a game of hide-and-seek, not only would he win every time, everyone would probably go home, forgetting that John was still hiding somewhere. It was hard to believe anyone would notice, even the next day.

In the year and a half since I transferred to the school, I'd never seen John anywhere except in the classroom, nor had I seen him enter a classroom. By the time I noticed, he was somehow already there, casting a faint shadow.

Only the teacher bothered a second glance. It would've been odd not to for all the racket he was making. Still, some students didn't bother to look at John even once. The boys especially. Maybe they feared catching the disease by looking at him.

Anyway, the teacher shot several looks at John. I happened to catch a glimpse of her face and felt absolutely horrible. Her eyes squinted as if they'd found a pesky tick living in the sheets. Then, as if to say, *I'm glad you're not my son*, she turned her back and carried on as if John wasn't there.

And so, class went on as usual. John cried louder. The world let out a hard laugh. John cried louder still. On the other side of the country, President Bush was sending troops into Iraq. On and on John went. At the same time, my idol, Michael Jackson, was arrested on child molestation charges. John let out a wail, smacking his hands on the floor as if to split it open. Still, the dung beetle went on rolling turds into balls. Yep, this world was too beautiful for words.

John thrashed and stamped, sending tremors across the floor like he was determined to put a crack in the earth. Ten minutes passed and, before he could achieve the epic feat, he stopped. Then, as if he'd wiped away the memory of being ignored, he began thumbing through the pages of the textbook. He stared at the diagram of the dissected rabbit. But he was done crying.

I felt sorry for him. Looking away, I stared at the clock and prayed for time to pass quickly.

Shoes

I sat on the floor of the open-air hallway where the student lockers stood. Even at a slow pace, it took less than two minutes to walk the hall from one end to the other.

I slipped on my headphones—they were barely held together with duct tape—and put on Radiohead's second album, *The Bends*. Then I went about my daily routine of watching shoes pass before me. Back and forth. Back and forth.

There was a strong smell of rain, perhaps because I was sitting near the courtyard. The damp, gloomy scent smelled like honey to me. The bottoms of people's shoes were wet, and the floor had become slick. But that, too, was normal.

It was only between June and August that Oregon didn't see rain. Apart from those summer months, it rained almost every day. I'd assumed the number of suicides in this state was especially high until I learned that it was even higher in Washington just up north.

I always planted myself on the floor anyway, paying no attention to how wet or grimy I got.

Although it wasn't rural enough to call it that, the high school was surrounded by enough green woods that it could hardly be considered a city school. If you rode the bus twenty minutes from the stop down the road, you would end up downtown with buildings and some brand name stores. But judging by the squirrels living in the trees by the school parking lot, you could hardly call the place a city—at least, not compared to where I came from.

Shopping options in town were limited, then limited even more by your musical preferences: hip-hop heads went looking for Adidas and Sean John, the skate punks went to Hot Topic, and so on. The only stores teenagers living off their parents' allowance could afford to go were the fast-fashion stores inside the mall or the indie shops always a heartbeat away from permanently shuttering their doors.

But you know what was weird? In a school of two hundred students, no two kids ever wore the same shoes. Believe me, I know. Everyone was always wearing different pairs. Which was why, even as I sat in front of my locker staring at shoes every morning, by the next day I forgot which shoes belonged to whom. Not surprising, considering I could count on one hand the number of kids who knew me by name and talked to me.

As I gazed at the shoes coming and going before me, a wood chip came flying at me from a distance. It skittered among the feet of students hurrying to their next class, trying to escape from being stomped on. Sadly, the struggle lasted only a few seconds, as the chip was crushed to smithereens by a black, studded boot. Seeing this made me terribly sad. My eyes chased after the boot bottom for a glimpse of a splintered corpse, but it disappeared from view.

Watching shoes go by day after day as I did, I learned that there was a certain style to the way they became dirty or worn. There was a difference between stylishly dirty and just plain dirty. If you examined the dirt on someone's shoes and the wearer's walk, you might get a sense of who that person was. The walk of someone wearing shoes that were just plain dirty, for instance, had no rhythm. He walked a bit adrift, his steps unsure, probably too conscious of his surroundings. The dirt on his shoes didn't get there by some purposeful action, but simply found itself there over the course of the wearer trying not to get in the way of others, careful not to get into any trouble. Someone with a stylishly dirty pair of shoes, on the other hand, planted one foot firmly in front of the other, heel first, all rhythm and confidence. The dirt looked like it had gotten there purposefully, not from exercise or from mere strolling, hinting at a fascinating story hidden beneath. When you saw a pair of dirty shoes, you either said, "You got some dirt on your shoes," or you asked, "How did you get them dirty?"— that was the simple difference.

I hardly knew anyone at the small school. And though I made a pastime of making fun of other people's shoes, I thought I was making a statement by writing "No

Fun"—the title of the last song the Sex Pistols ever per-
formed—on one side of my Converse in black marker.
On the other side was a drawing of a picture book character, making my shoes the most worthless pair in the
entire school.

They weren't so much dirty as discolored. No one
wearing shoes like these was likely to have much of a
story. However you looked at them, they were nothing
more than a ratty old pair of sneakers past their best-by
date.

So Long

As I passed the time in stone cold silence in a world all my own, Maggie came by and sat down next to me.

I could count the number of friends I had on one hand. I wasn't using all of my fingers, either. It was exactly one.

Maggie had green eyes.

She wrote something on a piece of paper and passed it to me.

What are you listening to?

I wrote my answer and passed the paper back to her.

The perfect song for a day like today.

Maggie read this, then turned the paper over and began writing. Giggling quietly to herself, she passed me the paper again.

What kind of day is it?

I got to my feet, pulled out a notebook from my locker, and sat back down next to her, so close that our shoulders touched.

Quiet and incredibly calm. How's your day?

Noisy. Too much noise inside my head.

Why? Did something happen?

Breaking up with boyfriend.

I looked up, and she gave me a helpless shrug. Then she went back to writing.

You're lucky. How I wish for a quiet and calm day.

I pointed to her pen as if to ask, *Can I?* and Maggie held it out on her palm. A steady rhythm of feet padded up and down the hall, crisscrossing before us.

I'm sad I won't be able to see you anymore. Today is my last day.

What do you mean last? Are you going somewhere?

Back to Japan.

Why? Something happen to your family?

My family's fine. I got expelled, that's all.

Maggie's mouth fell open. Her look reminded me of a deep-sea fish I saw once in a magazine.

But why? You haven't done anything.

I haven't. That's the problem, I wrote. *I haven't done a thing since I got here.*

Then start now. Isn't there something you can do?

Not anything that I want to do. It's okay. School isn't for me, that's all.

Maggie's eyes turned sad and filled with understanding.

That was Maggie. I could always tell her something, and she would probe the underside of my words, looking at me with those sympathetic eyes. She had a special way of understanding hopelessly twisted people. But that wasn't what was truly amazing about Maggie. What was truly amazing about Maggie was that she never formed into words what it was that she'd intuited or cast judgement on anyone. She always accepted things and people as they were. I loved Maggie with all my heart.

Then I don't want to stay in school either, she wrote. *You're the only one who doesn't mind talking to me like this. The other kids don't even bother.*

And then it was my turn to write.

Remember when we got yelled at in art class? What were we supposed to draw that day—a rainbow? Instead we wrote notes to each other until our papers were covered in ink on both sides. The look on Mrs. Pierce's face!

I kept writing in the notebook as Maggie laughed without making a sound. I held my sides and laughed silently along with her. I could have laughed out loud, but my voice left me when I was with Maggie.

A harsh bell sounded, tearing through our peaceful space.

Class is starting. Maggie could hear a little if the sound was loud enough, but I let her know just in case. *Don't you have class?*

Maybe I'll ditch! Maggie stuck out her tongue, then glanced secretively up and down the hall.

You can't! You'll get expelled!

I meant it half-jokingly, but Maggie's faced turned serious.

Less than six months away from graduation. How can they do this to you?

Maggie smacked a fist against her palm. It might have

been sign language of some sort, but I didn't care. What-ever it meant, the emotion was clear. Seeing Maggie angry made me happy and thankful that at least one person cared about my leaving. I didn't ever want to regret not telling her, so I wrote it down:

I feel lucky to have someone who cares. I'm sad, too, of course. Sad that I won't see you anymore.

Maggie peered at the page from the side as I wrote, reading as the words trailed out of my pen. Just as I'd finished writing, she lit up and threw up her arms. She grabbed the pen from my hand and began writing, swaying as if she were composing a song. While Maggie was writing, I got up and took out another pen from my locker.

Maggie tapped me on the knee twice as if to say, *Read! Read!*

I'm thinking of going to Alaska after graduation. You have to visit. We can see each other in Alaska!

Behind her glasses, Maggie's green eyes sparkled like emeralds.

Alaska! What if you get eaten by a bear?

Maggie elbowed me in the arm, then crossed her arms in front of her chest, shooting daggers at me with her eyes.

I'm kidding. Kidding!

I know that!

After writing this, Maggie held out a pinky finger.

She was asking me to pinky swear. I didn't want to make a promise I might not be able to keep, so I frowned and gave her a weak shrug. Maggie thrust out her pinky finger again. Again and again until I finally took it and squeezed. Until finally I promised to go to Alaska.

Satisfied, Maggie stood up, and after I did the same, she hugged me tight. Because we'd stood up from sitting shoulder to shoulder, I ended up in an awkward hug with a mouthful of hair and my arms locked at my sides, so I couldn't hug her back. Somehow I managed to bend my arms and swatted her on the back twice.

I pulled away for a moment and gave her another hug—a proper one this time. Wrapping my arms behind her back, I nearly started crying. Reluctantly, I took her by the shoulder and spun her in the other direction, then gave her a firm push toward the classrooms. Finally, with her shoulders sagging, Maggie started to walk. I sighed with a small sense of relief.

Aside from a few stragglers, the hall was empty. Maggie made her way down the hall between the rows of classroom doors and blue lockers without making a sound. No footsteps or squeaky shoes. She turned around only once. When our eyes found each other, we both managed a weak smile.

The receding figure of Maggie trudging to class reminded me of a certain red-nosed reindeer who was shunned from the rest of the herd. She looked miserable. But maybe she only looked that way to me because I felt so lonely. I grabbed a cigarette lighter out of my pocket and threw it, aiming for Maggie's shoulder. The lighter hit its mark. Maggie whipped around like she'd been shot with a peashooter.

"Alaska!" I said it out loud, worrying that my non-native tongue wouldn't be able to mouth the word clearly unless I did.

Maggie looked at me with those clear eyes, registering neither approval nor disapproval, and smiled. Her green eyes seemed to symbolize peace.

She picked up the lighter off the floor and threw it back at me. I caught it firmly with both hands.

"Alaska!" Although Maggie formed the word silently with her mouth, it came back at me loud and clear.

Choices

A heaviness hung in the air. Mr. Walker, the principal, occasionally heaved a theatrical sigh or cleared his throat. I didn't much enjoy silences between people in cramped spaces. The least he could do was put on some music. It didn't have to be rock music. As long as it was something—a hymn even—I wouldn't have complained.

The principal's office was the tiniest room in the school. Not including Mr. Walker sitting behind the desk, three more adults would fill the room entirely. Mr. Walker also taught classes, so he was rarely penned up in the tiny office. An old lady named Mrs. Miller managed all administrative duties.

The same Mrs. Miller, known as the real principal behind the scenes, was now surveying me from the chair nearest the door. I barely knew her, so this might as well have been our first meeting. She had short white hair, which was, either by birth or by design, curled into tight rings. If it was by design, she had good taste. She knew exactly the look that suited her. A tight perm on short hair? I wouldn't have had the courage.

Cradling several files in one arm, Mrs. Miller was busily writing down notes with the other. She seemed irritated, offering no opening for conversation. From the way she threw up a wall between herself and others, making her presence felt without saying a word, you just knew she wasn't a nice person. Watching her scribbling away gave me the illusion of being detained in a hospital or police station. Suddenly, I felt depressed.

Every little thing seemed staged. Fake. From the lazy sunlight spilling into the room to the potted plant decorating the windowsill, to the faded photograph of the school's first graduating class hanging on the wall— they looked like pieces of art staged for precisely this moment. The students in the photograph were dressed in blue robes, several of them proudly throwing their graduation caps high in the air, their gums bared in a mocking laugh. I sank into a deeper depression.

There was nothing to do but stare out the window. Raindrops dashed against the windowpane and trickled down the glass with a whimper. I'd seen that scene before. It hadn't been raindrops then but a dirty rag. But I guess that didn't matter now.

"Ginny," said Mr. Walker.

Was he calling my name? Yes, it was definitely my name.

"Is there something you'd like to say?" he asked, spreading out both hands, which had been clasped on the desk only a second ago. I felt like I was watching a Hollywood movie—which was disappointing because I'd grown sick of Hollywood movies lately.

I shook my head without attempting to fake regret.

"Are you sure?" Mr. Walker persisted. "This is it, Ginny."

Mrs. Miller turned over a page in her file.

Unable to bring myself to say out loud that I was, I nodded once.

"What would Stephanie say? Have you given any thought to that?"

"Stephanie?" I said.

"She's important to you, isn't she?"

He was right. Stephanie was very important to me. But what did that have to do with me getting expelled? I wasn't the one who had made that decision. He did. If Stephanie was going to be saddened at all, it was his fault. Was he trying to say that I was to blame?

What a pain in the neck. Although I wasn't about to give him the satisfaction of agreeing with him, I couldn't deny what he said. To be confronted with it felt terrible.

I propped an elbow on the armrest and clamped a hand over my mouth, which is what I always did when simply refusing to answer didn't seem like enough.

The principal cast a sympathetic eye toward me sitting there completely still, like the potted plant on the windowsill, breathing between my fingers. Mrs. Miller looked on with a cold expression.

"Very well. You may go home today," said Mr. Walker.

Today?

"Have a good talk with Stephanie."

About what?

"And if you still want to give up on school, well, then you will be dismissed. No take-backs. Once your dismissal is official, that will be the end. Do you understand, Ginny?"

Not. In. The. Least.

"What do you mean? You told me this morning that I was being expelled. What was that about?"

"I was hoping if you passed the morning thinking you'd already been expelled, maybe you would come to some sort of realization. This is your second chance. You will not be given a third. You get two chances, that's it."

As soon as the principal finished, Mrs. Miller's pen began to move faster. She scribbled furiously as if a new line of verse had come into her head.

"You can go now, Ginny. Come back when you've made your decision. But you have three days, not a day longer."

After that, I walked out of the principal's office.

Apparently, the story behind my ratty old sneakers was just a cringey comedy.

I stopped at my locker to get my book bag. The inside of most students' lockers were papered over with pictures and magazine clippings of famous people, but mine remained plain and its original blue. I slammed the locker door shut, sending a rusty rattle echoing across the empty hallway. For an instant, I locked eyes with Candace, who was on the cheerleading team, standing nearby. I walked away without so much as exchanging a smile with her.

Outside, the rain was coming down as usual. I pulled on the hood of my parka and started walking. The sky was endlessly ashen and gloomy. Every so often, the sun peered out from behind the clouds and gazed down at me.

I turned onto a busier road with a few cars, where there were more pedestrians wearing their hoods to shield the rain. With only the tip of the nose and mouth visible, they looked a bit like criminals trying not to be recognized. They all stared down at the rain pelting the asphalt, their hands pushed deep in their pockets. I warmed my cold-bitten hands inside my pockets too.

The rain was to blame for their downcast look— that's what the expression on their faces said. Maybe they were right. I'll be damned if any of us walking stone-faced beneath *this* sky had a purpose in life.

Stephanie

I'd been bounced around several schools—around the world, actually, from Tokyo to Hawaii to Oregon, before my host mother, Stephanie, took me in. It wasn't until some time later that I'd learned Stephanie was known around town as a famous picture book author. A Caldecott Medal-winning author no less. A sticker resembling an Olympic gold medal glittered on the cover of her picture book, *The Boy in the Hollow*.

Stephanie's house was littered with half-crumpled papers, not just in the workroom but all throughout the house. She had a habit of scribbling down ideas and images that came to her and promptly forgetting them, so scattered here and there were Nostradamus-like prophecies and cryptic pictures seemingly drawn by a gorilla or another highly intelligent animal. The first paper ball I'd picked up had this written on it: *The sky is about to fall. Where do you go?*

I looked up at the sky from the window. A shiver shook my body. The sky stretched forever and beyond. *This* sky about to fall? Where *do* you go?

I wasn't the type to take every little thing seriously, but this prophecy terrified me. I wandered around the house and searched for more balls of paper, in hopes of finding the answer. But I found none. Asking Stephanie was out of the question. If she found out that I was the kind of girl to steal a look at her work, even though she was the one who discarded it, she might have thrown me out before I could learn the answer.

Still, I couldn't help myself. I searched for more paper balls the next day and the day after. Exactly a week later, I found one behind the toilet. The crumpled paper was covered in dust. I picked it up off the floor and opened it. It was a drawing of what could be either a boy pixie or an alien. The expression on the boy's face was clouded as if my own face was being reflected back in a mirror.

Stephanie was always home. Some days she shut herself up in the workroom, coming out only to go to the bathroom, while on other days she roamed the living room all day like a lost child. On the roaming days, I made a point of staying home and reading, always in the living room. And there from behind my book, I watched her.

Sometimes she lit up with an idea, only to let out a disappointed moan a second later and hang her head. During these spells, Stephanie did not notice my presence. If the mountain behind the house sputtered black ash and swallowed us in darkness, or if the burnt ash and rain sent an evil, unearthly smell into the house, she wouldn't have noticed. It was as if Stephanie and I existed in another dimension. I didn't ever want to do anything to overstep the boundaries of our special place.

Maybe she'd seen me tramping around the woods behind the house. Or maybe she had decided to take a break from work. At times, Stephanie would say, "Why don't we go for a little walk," and take me out.

Our first walk together happened in late June—my first summer in Oregon after I'd been kicked out of a Catholic high school in Hawaii.

Stephanie drove us to the base of Mount Hood, which was blanketed in snow year-round. We went into a barn-like café that could easily be overlooked by non-locals and drank giant mugs of hot chocolate, breathing the faint smell of horses drifting in from somewhere. We spent close to an hour in silence.

These quiet periods with Stephanie were as pleasant as a breeze. And as natural as the empty mug in your hand after you've savored your hot chocolate to the last drop.

For our next walk, we went to the beach near the floating cave, which was a film location for the '80s movie *The Goonies*. We ate clam chowder and afterward, while we were walking around town, Stephanie said apologetically, "I'm sure it's nothing like the beaches in Hawaii." Actually, I preferred the beaches in Oregon so much more than the ones in Hawaii. The beaches on the islands, especially ones on Oahu, were overflowing with people, and when you wanted to enjoy a quiet walk alone, you were always getting accosted by drunk people. Being alone was impossible. The tourists painted the town red every night, the locals were trying to pick up the tourists, and as an Asian, I was constantly being harassed by both. At some point, when I'd wanted to spend some quiet time alone, I'd started going to the beachside tables where the homeless hung out. It was the only place no one bothered me. I loved listening to the sound of the men moving their chess pieces overlap with the crash of waves.

Among the homeless was an overweight woman confined to an electric wheelchair. The tires looked about ready to blow out at any moment. Plastic bags filled with dolls and sundries hung from the handles and the sides of the chair. Despite her appearance, the woman's voice was surprisingly gentle, and even quieter than the click-clack of the chess pieces. At night the homeless usually gathered around the same table and passed the time in cheerful chatter. Occasionally one man took to yelling at the tourists. The man was horribly skinny, his face sunken. Shabby shirt, beige pants. His feet were black with grime, and you could tell his fingernails stank just by looking at them. The man waved his arms, at times pointed at someone, and yelled, "You don't know nothing! Laugh if you want. Laugh if you think it's funny. But you don't know nothing!"

Even though I left Hawaii, I remember his words to this day.

Of course, if you went to the other side of the island, you wouldn't find a soul at night, and it was very quiet. But I didn't have a driver's license, and it was too dangerous for a girl to be out alone. So I spent many happy evenings alone by the safe and peaceful table among the homeless, staring at the ocean, listening to music, and writing in my diary.

The beach that Stephanie took me to was quiet, even during the day. You could see mountains ranging on either side of the majestic ocean, and a pleasant breeze was blowing. Every store in the lazy beach town seemed on the verge of going out of business, but when I opened the door to one shop and went in, the clerk greeted me with a great big smile. In my heart I apologized for worrying needlessly over their financial affairs. The shop sold mostly souvenirs, the shelves lined with magnets and painted seashells. And red gummy lips. Several middle school girls took turns holding the plastic-wrapped gummy up to their mouths, pointed at each other and giggled, and then took some pictures to remember the day. Still watching the girls from afar, I stopped in front of a terrarium with live hermit crabs. Someone had painted on their shells. I wondered whether the brushwork was to the crabs' liking, whether they'd had a good look at the design before moving into a new house. When I'd asked Stephanie, she said that they'd probably rather return to their real homes. *What is a real home?* I wondered. I thought about this for a while. Depression stole over me again, and I hardly spoke during the ride back.

Stephanie, still convinced that I disliked the Oregon beach, took me the next week to the train tracks the boys in the film *Stand by Me* had walked. Thanks to these outings with Stephanie, I fell for Oregon within three months of having moved there.

"Why do you hate Hawaii so much?" Stephanie once asked.

"What do you think of when you hear the word *Hawaii*?" I asked back.

"Oh, I don't know," she said, thinking. "Paradise?"

"Exactly. It's a twenty-four-hour party, all day, every day. Tourists visiting for a few days or a few weeks used to laugh at me and say, 'Hey, don't look so blue, you're in paradise!' The high school there had a similar vibe too. Maybe it wasn't quite like the tourists, but the classroom had this lazy mood, probably because it was so hot all the time. I worried that I'd get dumber if I stayed there. Everything moved so slow. It all felt like a lukewarm bath. I started out liking hula dancing, but before long I couldn't stand to watch it. I really grew to hate hula."

Stephanie tilted her head, listening.

"Anyway, I hated the overall vibe, like anyone who looked unhappy was just plain wrong. It was unnatural." Then I added, "Take a party, for instance. Of course, everyone goes to a party to have a good time, so that's all fine; but the fact that you're *expected* to have a good time felt, like I said, unnatural to me. But it was already too late. Even when I actually tried to have fun, it was too late. If you think I have a twisted personality, you're right. You're not going to get any argument from me. But the idea of someone being able to have a good time because someone told them to gave me the creeps. Sounds weird for me to say, I know, but Hawaii is hell for a misfit like me."

"I wouldn't say you're twisted. Maybe a tad dramatic."

I nodded. "Yeah, I guess."

"But I think I understand what you're saying," added Stephanie. "I don't much enjoy parties either. The way you're constantly being asked if you're having a good time. No one would ask in the first place, if you *looked* like you were having fun. And if you told them otherwise, you would just sound angry. Such a fuss. Although I doubt I'll be going to any of those parties anymore." Stephanie chuckled.

She must have been thinking about the dances the high school held several times a year. Of course, you wouldn't catch me at one of those things. It was much more fun listening to music in my underwear instead of one of those flashy, tight dresses, jumping up and down on my bed and dancing by myself. Stephanie said that if a boy asks, though, I should go. But no boy would ask me out anyway. First off, there wasn't anyone who knew me, anywhere. I didn't even qualify as a wallflower. I was invisible. Indeed, that was exactly what I aimed to be.

When I talked to Stephanie, I felt strangely at peace. I wondered if Stephanie might be invisible too. There were plenty of people who knew her, unlike me, yet no one seemed to know the real Stephanie. I suspected that Stephanie was hiding her true self. But I had found her. I had found her living quietly in the mountains, like she was avoiding discovery. Many times, I was tempted to yell in a voice that would ring clear on the other side of the globe, "Dragons are real! Dragons really do exist!" But I resisted because I could tell that she was a very delicate dragon with a sensitive heart. I couldn't reveal a secret like that so easily. Besides, the knowledge filled me with a tiny feeling of superiority.

For our last outing that summer, Stephanie said we were going to Multnomah Falls and drove us toward the mountains. From the narrow road that seemed to stretch forever, we could see the great Columbia River, which flows along the Oregon and Washington border. The road was called the Historic Columbia River Highway and was, I learned, designated an All-American Road by the Department of Transportation. The view was so magnificent that I lost the will to capture it with my camera. Instead, I was inspired and awestruck, swallowing my breath at every turn. The mere thought of there being a whole different state—Washington—on the other side of this perfect river made my heart race for some reason. And when a wild deer popped up on the side of the road, my heart nearly burst like a balloon. I stuck my body out of the car window and waved frantically. Keeping her eyes focused on the road, Stephanie scolded me to sit back down like I was a kindergartner.

We'd turned off at a square where several cars were stopped and parked the car. Stephanie threw up her arms and gave her stiff back a good, long stretch. Then she'd turned to me and said we were at the Vista House.

Stephanie and I looked out at the Columbia River and Washington beyond it. In the center of the parking area stood an old octagonal stone building that looked like a tiny castle or a lookout tower, or just the rooftop of one. The entrance was roped off with DO NOT ENTER tape. The building had impressively large windows and a roof the color of emerald stone. When I asked Stephanie what this place was called, she laughed and said, "This is the Vista House. Weren't you listening?"

I told her that it sure didn't *look* like a house.

After we'd circled the building, we stopped again and stood in awe of the river curving gently out from the misty clouds between the mountains. I tried to imagine the source of the river deep in the mountains and at once sensed the presence of something godly. In that moment, I envisioned a blob of water shaped like a head with its mouth open, unleashing a torrent that swallowed the mountains and clouds, the deer and flying birds—all of us—whole, washing us all away. The vision had sent a shiver up my spine. The magnificent view possessed the power to shatter your soul into a thousand pieces, put them back together in a different arrangement, and make you whole again.

We'd stood atop a cliff about 230 meters above the Columbia River. I looked across the water and spotted three deer drinking from the Washington side of the river.

I pointed them out to Stephanie, but her eyes were bad.

"My, you have sharp eyes," Stephanie said enviously.

I told her about the freight train chugging across the mountains.

"What kind of train is it?" Stephanie asked cheerily as if we were playing a game.

"The kind you see in a toy store, only smaller. A toy train more for an elf than a child. It's only as long as my pinky finger."

"Then it might be a bit large for an elf."

"Maybe."

According to Stephanie and me, elves measured five inches tall.

"The train is a lot smaller than one of those chew bones for small dogs, so there's probably nothing in it. I bet it's empty."

"Well, you never know. There may be a hundred tiny, tiny elves packed like sardines in that train."

"Packed . . . like sardines? Oh, like the long-distance trains in India or the trains in Tokyo during rush hours. People will click their tongue at you if your bag or shoulder bumps up against them even just a little."

"Oh dear."

"Stephanie? Why don't we stay here? Forget about the falls."

"No, we should go to Multnomah Falls."

"But why? This place is perfect."

"How can you know that? You haven't seen the falls yet! Come, we can stop here again on the way back. We'll be back this way anyway."

Stephanie ordered me back into the car, and we left the Vista House behind. We'd passed several cascades on our way to Multnomah Falls, each one more beautiful than the last. I carried on like a child, poking at leaves with a stick and throwing rocks at the ponds. Stephanie smiled and looked on, her eyes more maternal than my own mother's. I got carried away and threw a bunch of rocks at the basin of a waterfall, and Stephanie scolded me for angering the water.

Stephanie was right. Multnomah Falls turned out to be a wonderful waterfall. But as soon as Stephanie told me the legend surrounding it, my appreciation faded. Long ago (but when humans were already acting on vanity and rumors), a deadly sickness came over the tribe, and it was told that the sickness would be lifted if the daughter of a chief sacrificed her life to the Great Spirit. Unable to sacrifice any of the maidens gathered before him, his own daughter among them, the chief decided that no maiden would be sacrificed. Seeing how the tribe suffered, the chief's daughter slipped away at night and threw herself off the top of a cliff. When the chief found his daughter's body at the bottom of the cliff, he wept inconsolably. He prayed to the Great Spirit for a sign that his daughter had been welcomed into the spirit world. Then a stream of water came tumbling down from the edge of the cliff, and that was how this beautiful, slender waterfall came to be.

I liked legends, but really disliked this kind of legend. I put my hands together and offered a silent prayer to the daughter who had sacrificed her life for her people.

Afterward, I nagged Stephanie to go back to the Vista House until she shook her head wearily and pointed the car back in that direction.

When the sun started to set, and when our car was the only one left in the parking lot, we did not leave the Vista House. Stephanie and I sat on the roof of the car, let out lovestruck sighs, and in turn swallowed our breaths to savor the feeling. However many times you stared from edge to edge at the Columbia River, it was impossible to see the same view twice.

"Sorairo wa kokoro moyou," I murmured in Japanese.

"What?"

"The color of the sky is the shape of the heart. It means no view ever looks the same. And that's a good thing because that means your heart is never the same."

"What a lovely thing to say," said Stephanie.

The sky grew red and swirled into orange. Gradually, it turned purple, and as soon as a tint of pink crept in, just like that—the sky melted into a deep blue like the canvas of a fickle artist. And then the sky was completely dark, throwing the stars faintly into relief.

I thought about my friends in Japan.

As Stephanie and I gazed up at the sky, Stephanie asked, "Ginny, mind if I ask you a question?"

I made a slight nod. I sensed Stephanie's eyes on my cheek. "Yes?"

"Did something happen before you came here?"

"Something . . . like what?"

"I don't know. It's something I've noticed since we first met at the airport. You have very sad eyes."

"Sad eyes?"

"If you'd rather not talk about it, you can be honest and tell me so. It's just something I've felt."

"You're amazing," I said, being sincere.

"Something *did* happen."

I paused. "Maybe something did."

Maybe it was my vague answer. Stephanie stopped her questioning and went back to gazing at the stars. Then

she opened her mouth as if she'd remembered something. "It must have been hard."

"Mmm, probably."

"But you probably didn't cry very much," she said in a
gentle, coaxing manner.

"That's not true. I cried more than I want to admit."

"Oh."

"But yeah. I don't like crying all that much."

"Can I ask what I happened?"

"It was . . . something really, really small and yet really,
really big."

"Are you going to keep teasing?"

"I'm not. It's the truth."

"I understand. It's all right."

That was the last either of us said for a while.

A wind gusted between the mountains and up the
Columbia River, found us sitting atop the roof of the car,
tousled my hair, and swept past between us. When the
wind was gone, I felt empty, as though a hole had been
opened in my heart.

"I'm sorry. I've asked too many questions," said Stephanie a bit awkwardly. I wondered if she had been nudged
by the passing wind.

Slowly, I lowered my gaze to the dark-green roof of
the Vista House, then looked into Stephanie's eyes.
Unlike the Oregon sky, her eyes were a clearer kind
of gray, but in the dark, they were the same color as
mine.

"In Japan, there are two kinds of schools where
Japan-born Koreans like me can go," I began, tracing my

shoelaces with a finger. "You can go to a Japanese school, of course. And there are Korean schools: South Korean and North Korean. I used to go to a North Korean school. The one South Korean school in Tokyo mostly had Korea-born students and hardly any Japan-born Koreans going there. But the North Korean schools are where the Japan-born kids with Korean domicile status or South Korean citizenship went. I know it's confusing. Are you following so far?"

A tiny crease formed between Stephanie's brows. "Yes, I think so."

"There's so much that happened. I mean, really," I said. "I took down the portraits of Kim Il Sung and Kim Jong Il hanging in the classroom, smashed them to pieces, and threw them off the balcony."

Stephanie's breath caught in surprise.

"I've never told anyone the whole story. They told me I shouldn't. Even if they didn't, I don't think I could."

"Why's that?"

"What I did was wrong."

"Ginny, I'm sure I don't understand everything. But if what you say is true, then you must tell someone about it someday. Even if that someone isn't me. You must tell someone."

Could Stephanie be right? I looked up at the sky, pensive. Suddenly I remembered—

"The sky is about to fall," I said timidly.

Stephanie looked up at the sky. She appeared to be looking at neither the stars nor into the darkness. Her eyes seemed to be fixed on something much farther.

"The sky . . . about to fall? What a funny thing to say." She smiled knowingly.

"But if . . . the sky really did start to fall, where would you go?" I asked.

"This is the sky you're talking about. There's no escaping it. If the sky should ever fall, you must accept it and catch its fall. You mustn't run away," Stephanie said, as though the answer were obvious.

Stephanie's answer was a letdown. How was anything going to change by catching the sky's fall? The only sure thing to happen was that you were going to get crushed and die.

On the other hand, maybe Stephanie was right. Back when it felt as if the sky was falling, maybe I should have accepted it. Maybe I should have caught its fall.

Dear Paper—
A Confession

Some people say that a person who laughs a lot is a person who's been hurt a lot—that a genuinely kind person is someone who has deep wounds. But what if? What if that person is guilty of hurting countless others, more than they'd been hurt themselves? Can we really say that they're kind?

Someone who has used their own hurt as an excuse to hurt others, to betray, deceive, and drive away the people they care for most, throwing them into a dark abyss that they have to crawl on all fours to get out of.

That someone is me.

This is my story.

The wheels of my life started coming off five years ago. The story feels as distant as a past life, which is why the memories come to me in fragments. While I don't remember everything, something tells me I'm going to remember a lot of things today. Maybe being on the verge of getting expelled from school has something to do with it. I'm having terrible flashbacks. My head aches. I feel like I'm about to be sick. I don't care to know why, just as long as the random stream of images in my head stops. That's all I want, nothing more.

If someone were to read this, expecting to learn something from my story—not that anyone would—they'd be making a terrible mistake. I'll make that clear from the start. There isn't a single thing to be learned from what comes next.

First Day of School

April 1998. I set foot inside the gymnasium of Tokyo's largest North Korean school for the first time. I think it was a bright, crisp day, with the sweet scent of spring drifting in the air. I wouldn't go so far as to say the birds were chirping, but it wasn't raining—I remember that for certain.

The gymnasium might have been bigger than that of any school in Japan. It had second-tier stands, lined from end to end with red seats like a theater. When I turned to look up at the parents sitting in the seats looking down at us, I nearly forgot we were at school.

The black chima jeogori reminded me that we were in the middle of an entrance ceremony. Wearing the unfamiliar blouse and skirt made me itch. Thanks to the hemline, which barely exposed my ankles, I could spread my legs without giving the world an eyeful.

Kim Il Sung and Kim Jong Il beamed with pride. The scarlet curtains on the grand stage had been drawn back to reveal two enormous portraits of the Great Leaders.

To someone who'd transferred from a Japanese school like me, it was a strange sight to see.

The rest of the students, on the other hand, with whom I was about to be spending a lot of time, sat there, cool and collected. Apparently, I was the only one writhing inside.

One after the other, men in suits and women decked in colorful chima jeogori came up to the podium and delivered animated speeches punctuated with hand gestures, as if words alone couldn't possibly express the fabulousness of the day. Everyone else sat there, fixed with attention. I couldn't understand any of it. Everything was in Korean. I had a feeling that in another ten minutes or so, I would fall prey to deadly boredom and drowsiness. True to my prediction, I dropped off into a deep sleep.

The screech of chairs echoed across the gymnasium, startling me awake. I looked around to find everyone standing. I shot to my feet. The portraits of Kim Il Sung and Kim Jong Il were still hanging up front. Looking up at the Great Leaders, the students and teachers began to sing what I later learned was the school song. I stood there dumb, my mouth closed.

The song went on for four minutes, incomprehensible to me. When it ended, the gym erupted in applause.

And so began my life in junior high school.

An Unusual Class

"Go on. Introduce yourself to the class. Don't be shy."

Ms. Ryang, the seventh-grade homeroom teacher who wore a bright pink-and-yellow chima jeogori, spoke to me in a mix of Japanese and Korean.

I stood in front of the class, dreading how I was about to make a complete fool out of myself.

Every eye in the classroom locked onto my face. Their gazes were not warm. They stared at me like they were eyeing an antique, trying to appraise whether it was truly valuable or just another hunk of junk.

I wanted to leave right there and then.

"My name is Pak Jinhee. I came from a Japanese school. Nice to meet you." I introduced myself with the few Korean words I'd learned, prompting a few uninspired claps. I peered up at the teacher's face, expecting her to take control of the situation. Paying no mind to my humiliation, Ms. Ryang put on a happy face. She gave me several slow claps as if to say, *Good job!*

"Jinhee is new to Korean school, so she isn't able to

speak our language. Until she can understand Korean, we will conduct class in Japanese. I hope you will help her, so she can learn the language quickly. All right, class?"

When Ms. Ryang finished, the students answered, "*Yea,*" in unison. A couple of students shot me a surly look. I dropped my head and looked away.

I hate this. Not only were the words written on my face, I also nearly blurted them out.

It was forbidden to speak Japanese in Korean school. Now the whole class was required to speak in Japanese because of me. It was the worst possible start to my new life in junior high school.

Scene 3:
The Cycle of Prejudice

INT. CLASSROOM - DAY

The classroom is buzzing with postlunch chatter.

Jaehwan takes out a textbook from his book bag and is putting it away in his desk when—

>   YUNMI
> Some girl just transferred here from
> a Japanese school.

Yunmi sits on the edge of Jaehwan's desk.

>   JAEHWAN
> Yeah, so?

>   YUNMI
> I heard Japanese schools are brutal.

JAEHWAN

It's school. They're all the same.

Jaehwan slides Yunmi off the desk with a palm.

YUNMI

I heard Japanese school kids are
stuck-up.

JAEHWAN

And *we're* so pure and innocent? Don't
let her get to you.

YUNMI

There's something not right about
her. The way she looks at us like
we're monkeys or something. Maybe
someone needs to give her a good
scare.

JAEHWAN

Don't.

YUNMI

Why not? I'm only saying just a
little. Someone needs to teach her a
lesson before she starts acting all
high-and-mighty because she came from
a Japanese school.

JAEHWAN

Don't you have anything better to do?
Whatever. Leave me out of it.

Nina

"Here, Jinhee. I thought maybe you could use this."

A girl with a grown-up look about her named Nina gave me some handwritten charts of the Korean alphabet. She had tidy features and shiny hair gathered into a bun on top of her head. I stared at the wisps hanging over her ears, thinking how soft and delicate her hair looked.

Nina spread the charts out over my desk. The truth was I already knew the Korean alphabet. A teacher had been coming to my house every Saturday since elementary school to teach me the basics. I decided to accept Nina's kind gesture and said nothing. In fact, I felt deeply grateful, especially since I'd worried I was nothing more than a nuisance to my new classmates.

Nina smoothed out the handmade charts with a satisfied look of accomplishment. She sat down at the desk in front of me and watched me staring at the charts. "If there's anything you don't understand, you can ask me anytime." She smiled at me sweetly.

"Thanks."

"Hey, can I ask you something?"

"Yeah?"

"Japanese school—what was it like?"

"What was it like?" I echoed. "How do you mean?"

"Was it scary? I mean, were you bullied or discriminated—?" The last part came out like a gasp.

"Not really." I lied.

"Oh, was it fun?" Nina smiled.

"Sure."

"Oh, good. I hope Korean school is going to be fun for you too."

"Yeah."

I hoped so too. I really did.

From the day I entered Japanese school as a Zainichi Korean born in Japan, I was faced with a choice. A simple choice to make but incredibly difficult to pull off, whichever the choice.

Grow up faster than anyone else, or turn rebellious like other kids.

I chose to grow up. I didn't have a choice really. If you acted wild, you were always going to be the one who got blamed. If you acted wild, even if it was because you'd experienced some kind of discrimination, it was all over for you.

Letter from North Korea 1

Dearest Daughter,

Hello, Aelin. I hope you are well. I am doing fine. Three years have passed in the blink of an eye. The days pass so quickly that sometimes I forget to stand still. North Korea is a very comfortable place to live. It wasn't easy leaving Japan, but coming here was the right to thing do. The country is developing by the day. There is construction going on everywhere, so there isn't any time off from work. As soon as I get home, I fall down like a dead man and drop to sleep before I can eat. Still, I know I have found a job worth doing. I had hard work in Japan too, so there's nothing to it. Besides, the laborers work equally here. Compared to what it was like in Japan, there's nothing to it. It pains me to not be able to see your face and hold you. Take good care of yourself. I hope we will see each other again. How I wish we could see each other again. Eat well and sleep well, and take good care. I will write you again. Until then, goodbye for now. I miss you every day.

Your Father

Nugu?

There was this boy named Jaehwan.

He was one of a gang of amoeba-brained boys always making a loud entrance, as if they owned the class. If that wasn't bad enough, he was the only member of the boxing club. He was, I thought, one of those stupid boys who wanted only to talk with his fists.

One very sunny day during lunch period after everyone had eaten their bentos, the classroom was noisy with chatter and clatter, but because everyone was talking in Korean, I couldn't join the conversation. To be honest, there were moments when I felt sad sitting alone among the students laughing and clowning around, so on that day, I snuck out and went to the music room. The room had a grand piano for anyone to play. At least, there weren't any signs forbidding it. I took that as an invitation to play whenever I pleased.

As soon as I closed the door behind me, I felt instant relief. There was no one in the room, which was empty save the piano. As terribly bare as it was, I felt at home within a minute.

I sat down on the piano bench and pressed a key with a finger. The sound that came out was neither too high nor too low—how should I describe it? It was a light sound, at once bland yet thrilling, somewhat comical too. I struck a different key next. Then, with both hands on the keyboard, I pressed down on several keys at the same time, which cheered me up. Before I knew it, I was banging away on the piano with total abandon.

There wasn't a single song I knew how to play. I was only fooling around, hitting the keys at random. Yet, at times here and there, my fingers stumbled onto a melody that might've actually turned into a masterpiece. Drunk on the possibility of becoming a composer, I went on pounding away at the piano.

The door rattled open.

I started as though roused out of a dream and shot a look at the door to find Jaehwan standing there. I jumped away from the piano bench. My cheeks flushed. Had I been playing normally, I wouldn't have thought anything about being seen, but I'd been banging on the keys like a girl possessed. *This can't be happening!* I screamed to myself. *How do I talk myself out of this one? I just want to die!*

I expected him to run back to the classroom and tell everyone that I'd completely lost it. I didn't care. I just wanted him to go away.

Staring fixedly at my face, Jaehwan took one step closer, and then another, until he was standing in front of me.

There was an awkward silence. Neither of us said a

word. If a pencil were dropped, it would have sounded like a spectacular crash. The air drifting between us seemed to command us to not look away. My mind was blank, and at the same time incredibly noisy, as if a million parasites were shrieking in my brain.

Jaehwan was the one who broke the silence.

"*Nugu?*" he said.

"*Nugu?*" I echoed quizzically.

Jaehwan nodded. Then he said it again. "*Nugu?*"

Take it off? What's he trying to say? Does he want to strip or something?

Jaehwan belonged to the boxing club. Maybe he wanted to take off his shirt to show off his muscles. Or was he telling me to take mine off?

Was he stupid or something?

I took a step back. Then another. Jaehwan stood there, stunned, making no effort to move. Now was my chance. I gave Jaehwan the slip and made a dash for the door.

"Hey!" he shouted. I kept on running.

I bolted out of the music room and raced up the staircase on the right. Three girls whose faces I didn't recognize were coming down the stairs, goofing off in Korean. I blew up the stairs between them, and a tiny scream went up. One of the girls barked "*Ya!*" but I didn't slow down to apologize. I didn't dare. It was only after I'd reached the top step of the stairs that I turned around. Jaehwan didn't appear to be chasing me.

I couldn't bring myself to calm down. My heart was drumming uncontrollably. I searched the classroom for

Nina and found her chatting with some other girls out on the balcony. I ran out and shouted, "Nina!"

I must have looked as if I'd seen a ghost as Nina, looking shocked, asked, "What's wrong? What happened?" Everyone on the balcony was straining their ears to hear.

"Jaehwan said *nugu*."

"What?"

"I was in the music room, and he said *nugu* and came up to me."

"And?"

"And?" I repeated.

"And what did you do?"

"I got out of there, what do you think I did?" I said flatly.

"Why? Why didn't you just tell him your name?"

"Huh?"

"Why did you run away? All he was asking was your name," said Nina.

Dumbfounded, I tried to sort out what had happened. It took about a minute to register that *nugu* meant to take something off in Japanese, and *nugunya* meant "who are you?" in Korean.

So basically, what I did was slap the label of *class weirdo* on my forehead.

Jaehwan must have sniffed us out gossiping about him because he came out onto the balcony. "What's with you?" he asked, with a look of irritation. The Korean was simple enough that even I could understand. Then why didn't I understand a question as basic as "who are you?"

I cursed myself and the Korean tutor who came to my house every Saturday.

"What? I don't understand what you're saying," I said to Jaehwan, as if that would cast off my shame. Then I turned around and walked away.

"Did you see the way she was?" said a girl's voice behind me.

The voice belonged to Yunmi.

Silent Treatment

Two months passed. Although classes were still conducted in Japanese and the tests given to me came with translations, gradually I got used to the way things were in Korean school and opened up to Nina quite a bit.

One afternoon during homeroom, Yunmi raised her hand and announced to the entire class, "Jinhee hasn't tried to use Korean at all. Nina has been helping her learn, but she hasn't made any effort to speak a word of Korean."

That was a lie. When I got angry, I would correctly shout "Ya!"

"We're all trying to help, but if Jinhee isn't going to try, I think we should go back to having class in Korean."

On this, we were in agreement. I had wanted to propose going back to Korean too. But Ms. Ryang pointed out that, seeing how it's only been two months, perhaps as a friend, Yunmi might like to support me for a while longer. After sitting back down sourly, Yunmi shot me a glare when no one was looking.

The Korean school was always putting on group events and activities. Students were gathered in the gymnasium and brought onto the stage by grade to sing songs. We wore red neckties—more like kerchiefs, actually—and marched in a circle around the athletic field. I liked red, and I liked neckties, but I hated marching. I made a point of not asking why we were being made to march in the first place. Something told me it wasn't anything I needed to know. If I did, I had a feeling I'd break formation and make a run for it.

It was like Yunmi said: I wasn't making any effort. I didn't learn the school song, so when everyone else was singing, I either kept my mouth clamped shut, or opened and closed my mouth like a goldfish. That is, until Nina printed out the lyrics and wrote down the correct pronunciation for me.

After the incident, Jaehwan started coming around every day to talk to me. I ignored him, of course, but the enemy was relentless. He made a game out of saying something that might get an answer out of me. When he got tired of being snubbed, he pinched the collar of his dress shirt, mugging a face.

"Nugu?" The boy had way too much time on his hands.

One day during break, I was letting Nina listen to Hikaru Utada's "Automatic" on my Walkman. Since the radio was only starting to play her music, few people knew who Hikaru Utada was. I wanted Nina to hear the song first before I let anyone else listen as a small way to pay her back for all her kindness. Then Jaehwan showed up and said teasingly, "Annyeonghasimnikka!"

I shot him a dirty look and growled, "Go away."

That was when Yunmi, with her nostrils flaring, shouted "Ha! Showing your true colors at last!" and slammed both hands on my desk.

"What do you think?" I asked Nina, pretending not to hear Yunmi.

"Don't ignore me!"

"Hmm, I don't know. I guess it's all right," Nina said, taking off the earphones.

Yunmi yelled "Nina!" then shouted more things in Korean.

"How can you not love this?" I said to Nina. "I have this song literally on repeat."

"You! Jinhee! Pak Jinhee!" Yunmi kept on shouting.

She was a persistent one. I shrugged and threw her an annoyed look.

"You're not fooling me," Yunmi said. "I'll make sure everyone knows what you really are."

I waved her off as if to say, *Good luck with that.*

A few days later, I was letting Nina listen to the Spice Girls' first album, when Yunmi showed up with a bunch of boys from the class next door.

Yunmi said something in Korean, and all the boys turned their eyes on me. There were about ten of them. I had to cut my conversation with Nina short to keep an eye on them. Since the lead boy was blocking the doorway, some of the others were peeking in from the hall, standing on their tippy toes.

Now what? I got up from my chair.

When Yunmi pointed at me and said something again,

the boys laughed scornfully and began stretching their necks, rotating their wrists, and cracking their knuckles like they were gearing up for a fight. But after a few minutes, they all crowded out of the classroom.

I didn't know what to make of it. Yunmi was snickering with a smug look of satisfaction.

"Don't pay attention to her," said Nina reassuringly.

I didn't pay Yunmi any attention at all.

Things took a turn during cleaning period when Hyangeun came and found me in the girl's bathroom. "Yunmi told Nina that if she stays friends with you, the whole seventh-grade class will give her the silent treatment!"

"Where? When?" I asked.

"Just now, in the classroom. She threw water on Nina," said Hyangeun.

It was then that I remembered the choice: grow up faster than anyone else, or turn rebellious like other kids. This was a Korean school, not a Japanese school. I didn't have to worry about being singled out for being Korean, or being the only Korean in everyone else's eyes because, here, we were all the same ethnicity. For the first time, I felt an unshakeable freedom. I decided right then and there to spread my wings as far as they would stretch.

I grabbed my mop and made to leave the girls' bathroom. On my way out, I thanked Hyangeun for coming to tell me. I told her on the way out because I thought it'd come off cooler that way. I was invincible. With the mophead dangling behind me, I rested the handle on one shoulder like a wooden sword and marched down the middle of the hallway past the eighth-grade classrooms.

"What's going on, Jinhee? Out on a date with your mop?" one senpai asked amusedly.

When I answered "Whatever," stone-faced, he and his friends cleared a path for me to pass.

I spotted one of my classmates, with the lucky-sounding name. "Changsoo, have you seen Yunmi?"

"No, I haven't."

"You must've seen her. Think."

Changsoo eyed me and the mop suspiciously. "What are you up to?"

"She's out to expose me."

"What? Who?"

"Yunmi wants to expose me for who I really am. So, I guess I'm going to show her. Will you tell her that when you see her?"

"Okay. I'll tell her."

I smiled. I remembered to thank him in parting. Hoisting the mop on my shoulder, I went on the hunt for Yunmi. Not one person would tell me where she was. The bell rang. It was a shame, really. It wasn't like I had any real intention of doing anything with the mop. Besides, there was no way the entire seventh-grade class would go through with giving cheerful, gentle Nina (who was also popular with the boys) the silent treatment.

My heart danced at the thought of what Yunmi might try next to torment me and what I might do to get back at her. But the bullying stopped that day.

It seemed like Changsoo's luck had smiled upon not me, but Yunmi. After I'd left him, Changsoo had run into Yunmi and cautioned her to stop.

Yunmi stopped messing with me. In fact, she stopped talking to me altogether. When we ran into each other in the girls' room or locked eyes in the halls, even when no one else was around, we didn't talk. Once in a while, Hyangeun would give me a detailed account of how Yunmi had said this or that about me, but I couldn't bring myself to care anymore. As long as things quieted down, I was all right with that.

That was what I told myself to try and make it so.

Koreans, Get Out

Before I enrolled in the Korean school, I went to a Japanese school for six years, with a Japanese first name. I vaguely knew about the existence of Korean schools in Japan from my relatives. Having never been taught anything about ethnic consciousness or Korean culture, I knew about the schools in name only. But I'd heard enough to know that Korean, not Japanese, was spoken on school grounds.

Back in elementary school, every time I spotted a right-wing van—the ones with the loudspeakers blaring nationalistic propaganda—I tried to hide my ethnicity in my school uniform. Since I attended a private school, we all wore the same uniform. We also had similar facial features. Black hair, flat nose—some had monolids, while others had double lids, sure, but there wasn't all that much difference between us. I could blend in among my friends and make myself disappear.

That didn't mean that I concealed my identity. Since I went by my Korean last name, everyone knew I wasn't Japanese. Back then, I got along with others and made friends pretty naturally. I'd never told any of my friends about my fear of the right-wing vans, though. They only thought of the vans as noisy nuisances. Thanks to them, I'd come to think of the vans as nothing more than nuisances too. Soon, I became unafraid of making eye contact with the right-wing protesters giving hateful speeches.

At some point, I'd started to make a game of it. *Can you find me?* I muttered in my head. I felt as though I was Waldo, or that I was challenging the right-wing protesters to find the mistake.

Find the one mistake in this picture. Who is it? What is it? Can you find it?

"Koreans, get out! Koreans, go back!" shouted the protesters.

Cloaked in my uniform, I smiled at one protester standing next to the van. He made a quizzical face and looked away.

The elementary school I attended was an escalator school, which continued up to high school, so most of the students spent the twelve years until graduation with the same groups of friends. But not me. I would be going to a Korean junior high school, and had told everyone so, just as naturally as I'd been about not hiding my ethnicity.

In sixth-grade history class, when it came time to talk about Japan's colonization of the Korean Peninsula, I became nervous for some reason. Then, the teacher read aloud the few lines covering the history of colonized Korea in the textbook and added, "I guess this concerns people like Pak-san." The eyes of the entire class landed on me. Not knowing how to react, I stuck out my tongue and let out a lame chuckle. Thus, the lesson on the history *concerning me* ended in a matter of minutes.

A few days later during recess, a girl named Iguchi with long hair like Sailor Moon but not nearly as well-liked as the anime character, stood in front of my desk and stared at me like she was studying an insect. Then, without saying a word, she left. Iguchi was a bit of an odd bird, the kind that talked about the ghosts she'd seen the night before. But given how I'd been called *quirky* and treated like an oddball myself, I felt a kinship with her. That was why I wasn't all that bothered—a bit curious, maybe—about her giving me the long stare.

That same day on my way home from school, I spotted Iguchi on the train platform and asked if she wanted to go home together. She ignored me. When she made to leave, I tugged on her arm, and she spun around and shouted, "Get your dirty hands off of me!"

Oh, so my hands are dirty, I thought, turning my hands over to check them. There wasn't any noticeable dirt that I could see.

Iguchi gave a scornful snort. "Are you stupid or something? Get away from me, Korean." With that, she walked off toward the other end of the platform.

My good friends came up behind me soon after. They asked what Iguchi had said to me, so I told them. They talked trash about Iguchi to try to cheer me up. After feeling a little better, I rode the train, joking about this and that with my friends. But once I was home, the thought of Iguchi crept into my mind.

Umma found me before dinner, sitting on the shelf decorated with framed pictures, scratching at the wood grain. "What's wrong, what happened?" she asked.

"Iguchi said I had dirty hands."

"Were your hands dirty? What were you doing?"

"She called me a Korean."

With that, Umma seemed to infer everything and sat down next to me on the shelf. Since she was always yelling at me not to sit there, I could sense, as young as I was, that we were about to have a serious talk.

"What do you think, Jinhee? Do you think Koreans are dirty?" she asked.

"Of course not."

"What if you asked her why she would say such a thing, why she thought so?"

I thought about it, but I didn't want to ask. If I did, what was I supposed to do with the answer? What was I supposed to do if it wasn't the answer I wanted to hear?

Noting my troubled face, Umma continued, "I doubt your friend has an answer. She probably said it because she doesn't know anything."

As I ate dinner, the girl's face reentered my mind. Suddenly, I felt anger rising from inside me. My hands *weren't* dirty!

And then, as if she'd read my mind, Umma said, "You mustn't try to get back at her, do you hear me? Promise me you'll do nothing."

Umma made me swear, so I was stuck. Nevertheless, that word Iguchi spat out—*Korean*—had not only stayed with me, but likely with my friends too. And so, whenever someone asked me about Korean school, I made a point of explaining plainly, "It's a place where Koreans like me go"—short and sweet, the way the history teacher had tried to explain my history.

Iguchi went around telling everyone at school what her parents had told her—that I would have to wear a chima jeogori because that was the kind of place Korean school was. My friends stopped asking me about the school I'd be attending. They started to keep their distance from me and kept me at arm's length. The history teacher looked at me like he was eyeing a criminal. Whenever he walked past my desk, or we passed each other on the stairs, he threw me a look that felt to me like hate.

It's a place where Koreans like me go. I wished I'd never said it.

It was just that I didn't know anything about anything back then.

The Portraits in the Classroom

One day, before the start of summer break, during afternoon cleaning period, the portraits of Kim Il Sung and Kim Jong Il caught my notice, not as a part of the daily scenery, but as an eyesore I could no longer ignore. The very sight of them creeped me out, so I began to throw the dirty rag I'd been using to clean the floor at the portraits, again and again.

At some point, I went into autopilot mode and kept on making target practice out of the portraits. Some of the boys in the class laughed, but most of the other students were horrified by my recklessness and couldn't hide their shock. The classroom fell dead silent. Somehow, I'd completely missed my chance to stop. So on and on I went throwing the rag, picking it up, and throwing it again. It was Yunmi who gave me an escape.

"Jinhee!" she shouted upon entering the classroom. It was the first time she'd spoken to me since the mop incident. The rag smacked the portrait of Kim Il Sung across the face and fell disappointedly on the floor.

"Don't," Yunmi said under her breath in Korean.

Her voice was so soft that it was nearly drowned out by the swish of brooms sweeping out in the hallway. Yunmi said nothing more, and I didn't offer anything in response. Yunmi's face, which was pale to begin with, looked even paler, and I knew I had done something I shouldn't have. Her face was more convincing than anything she could have said. What I had done didn't reach anyone else's ears. None of the students ratted me out to the teachers. It remained a secret among those who happened to be in the classroom. Well, not a secret so much as something that was swept under the rug. No one came to question me later. But from that day on, I couldn't look at the portraits as simply a part of the scenery anymore. Just as I had stood before the right-wing van, whispering, *Find the mistake in this picture*, the portraits of the two Kims were now whispering to me, *There is a mistake in this classroom. Can you find it?*

I searched for the mistake all during class. *Something's not right. What? Where? How?* I searched high and low for the error.

"Okay, Jinhee. See if you can solve this problem," said the creepy math teacher standing at the blackboard. He must have thought that I was staring at him instead of at the portraits above the blackboard.

"I don't know," I answered honestly, in Korean.

"Why don't you give it a try?"

The guy was persistent. He'd said *try* in English and the rest in Korean. Although speaking in Japanese was forbidden at the school, English was allowed.

"I said, I don't know! Leave me alone," I said in Japanese.

The teacher grabbed me by the scruff of the neck and tossed me out of the classroom. It was a scene the rest of the class had seen many times before. No big deal. That was just Jinhee being Jinhee.

Two weeks passed, and I still couldn't find the mistake. I was irritated. School went on, and then, exam period. I filled in every blank on every test with *Kim Il Sung* or *Kim Jong Il* and turned them in.

Of course, I got caught.

I was taken to the teachers' room and asked a bunch of questions. Since I failed to answer any of them properly, I was made to sit on my knees in a proper seiza for about an hour on the balcony outside the teachers' room. As my legs went numb, I realized there was no point in suffering through this. I had nothing to protect, after all. My punishment wasn't anything but empty suffering.

"I couldn't understand, that's all," I said. "I couldn't understand the questions, so I wrote what I could."

After I made this confession, the creepy math teacher let out a heavy sigh and said, "Let's work harder on learning Korean," and let me go.

Letter from North Korea 2

Dearest Daughter,

It has been too long since my last letter. I'm sorry. I wanted to write you right away, but so much has happened. Really, so much that I couldn't write you until now. I am sorry about that. How are you doing, Aelin? You've had your baby. Congratulations. I wish I could have gone to the hospital and held the little one, the newest member of the family, in my arms. Although that's unlikely to happen now, it would make me very happy if you would send me a picture of her. One picture will do. If you happen to take one, please do send it to me. You've given her a good name. Did you decide the name with your husband? I can't ask you to visit me in North Korea when she is older. It seems unlikely that I will be able to leave this place. Take good care of your family. I know these words may ring hollow, but I do love you, Aelin. And your new family. Jinhee—it's a beautiful name. She will grow up well, I know it. That is why you must think only of your family from now on. Forget about me. Do you understand? Please, do not expect any more letters. Lastly, I'm sorry for everything. I love you. I love you from the bottom of my heart. If that is all you remember, I will not want for anything more. Thank you for being a daughter to this hopeless father.

Your Father

For the Love of a Cheese Dog

I fell head over heels for him. It all started because I was hungry.

The bento that Umma made wasn't enough to fill me up, so I took a walk over to the new cafeteria in the high school building to buy a cheese dog. As I stood in line, a group of older girls cut in front of me. Thinking they didn't see me, I said, "Excuse me," but the girls made a face as one might at a fly buzzing in their ear and ignored me. The snub was so cold and perfect that under different circumstances, I might have complimented them. Instead, I lost my cool and clicked my tongue. There were three of them. The ponytailed girls turned toward me in unison and glared, each of their faces resembling a horse's ass.

I blurted, "What are you swamp trolls looking at?"

Now why did I have to go and say that? Yeah, I had a big attitude, but I was really a chicken at heart. My heart pounded so hard I thought it might explode. I tried to put up a calm front, crossing my arms across my chest to hide my nervousness. But the girls didn't come back at me. They let the whole thing drop. They weren't the slightest bit interested, apparently, in the senseless yipping of a junior high schooler. They had acted like perfect adults.

I went away impressed, apologetic even, until a couple of days later the girls showed up at the junior high building to snitch on me. Though they didn't know my name, the teachers, including Ms. Ryang, all helpfully pointed their fingers at me at the same time.

The whole thing blew up into a bigger mess than expected, and a tedious discussion, with Ms. Ryang mediating, took place over several hours, and we were basically told to shake hands and make up. Since neither side was satisfied by this demand, the handshake never happened. Far from it, actually. I clicked my tongue again and again. *Whatever.* The fact that I'd managed to get the attention of some high school girls had gotten me all worked up.

That day on my way home from school, about ten girls from the high school surrounded me. I instantly regretted my cocky attitude from earlier. As the girls edged closer, they made a show of swinging their arms and cracking their knuckles.

Although I was always picking a fight, I'd never actually been in one before. I didn't know what it felt like to get hit. *Oh, God, this is gonna hurt, please don't punch me in the face, the stomach would be so much better, I hope they take it easy on me, I don't like this, I wonder if they'd listen if I asked them to spare the face.* These were the thoughts whirling in my head. Then, Jaehwan showed up. He appeared to me in that moment like a prince. He'd been teasing me nonstop until then, but here he was now to rescue me!

But no. He pointed at me from a safe distance and laughed. I gave him an urgent look, but Jaehwan made like De Niro and shrugged with his arms spread in front of him. Like, *What are you gonna do?*

"Who do you think you are, you little brat!" said one of the girls, cracking her knuckles.

Here we go, I thought, and then—Jaehwan left his perch from the sideline and strolled toward us with a bag of popcorn in his hand.

"Excuse me," he said in Korean, stopping at my side, then asked the older girls politely, "Is something going on here?"

"Nuguya? This isn't about you. Leave."

I almost broke out laughing at hearing *nugu* being shouted at Jaehwan.

"I can't exactly do that. Jinhee and I are in the same class, and she'll never let me hear the end of it if I leave her here," he said, switching to Japanese.

"Haah?" The girl's voice came out of her mouth like a fart.

"She's a troublemaker in class, so I'm sure she's done something pretty bad to—"

"Talk Korean," shouted another horse's ass in Korean.

Jaehwan pulled an overly apologetic face. I wanted to warn him off doing so, fearing that, contrary to its intended effect, it might piss them off even more, but he kept on bobbing his head.

"The problem is she won't understand if we speak

in Korean. I see why you'd want to beat her up. Sometimes, I want to pummel her myself, the way she's always ignoring me when I say hi to her. Really, sometimes I just want to punch her lights out. But you know, even though she may look like she's got a pair of balls on her, she *is* a girl. So if you want to hit her, you might as well hit me instead."

"What's the point of hitting you?"

I was thinking exactly the same thing.

"Forget it, just go away," I said quickly, but Jaehwan ignored me. "Go away, I said."

"Say you're sorry," he said.

"What?"

"I said, say you're sorry."

"What for?"

"It's your fault."

"No, it's not."

"Of course it is. Look at all these people surrounding you."

Jaehwan was right. How did I get here? As hard as it was to believe, when Jaehwan put it that way, I started to feel that maybe it was my fault. Despite trying to convince myself otherwise, feelings of doubt kept creeping in.

"Hmm . . ."

"See, you did do something."

"Maybe a little." I felt my cheeks blush. Not because I answered in Korean, but because I was bashful about being honest. I gestured "a little," pinching my two fingers together to hide my embarrassment.

"Now say you're sorry." Jaehwan was half smiling. Did I just make him smile?

"You two can't be serious," said one of the girls.

I wanted to come back at her with something sarcastic, but I kept my mouth shut.

"Very serious," Jaehwan answered, with a straight face.

The girls waited for me to apologize. No one wanted to hit Jaehwan, an innocent bystander. But if one of them hit me, and Jaehwan did the unthinkable and started swinging, none of them wanted to take a punch from a boy, even if he was a few years younger. I decided, reluctantly, to apologize.

"Sorry."

"We can't hear you."

"Sorry!" I said, louder this time.

"Do it the right way," the girls said in unison.

Jaehwan nudged me with his elbow. *Do it already!*

I accepted my defeat at last. I said, "I'm sorry," in Korean this time, and bowed my head the way my kindergarten teacher had taught me to greet the school bus driver every morning.

"Don't come around the cafeteria again," one girl spat out, and the high school girls straggled off in the direction of the train station. The ending was kind of a letdown.

"You owe me, you know that," said Jaehwan.

"Oh, yeah, sure."

"Don't *yeah, sure* me. You were about to get beat up by a bunch of girls."

I let out a chuckle.

"This isn't funny."

"Thanks."

"You don't mean that."

"Sure, I do."

"I don't know . . ." Jaehwan acted as if he was talking to a Pinocchio warped beyond redeeming. And my nose wasn't growing or anything. "You better not go back to the cafeteria."

"Sure, if I don't get hungry."

"Then don't get hungry."

"I told them I was sorry, so it's okay now."

"It's not okay."

"If they try to do anything to me again, it wouldn't be my fault. Besides, they're in high school. They're a lot more grown up than I am."

"Shut up," said Jaehwan. He was smiling.

A gentle, kind smile. Why didn't I know he could smile like this before?

He was smiling all during the walk to the train station. Gazing at his profile, I felt somehow calmer and dizzy at the same time. The odd thing was I also felt like I might drift off to sleep. In a million years, I could never be like Jaehwan. What had I seen in him before? Maybe nothing. Looking at him now, I realized he had clear, still eyes. I wished those eyes would go on looking at me for as long as possible.

Taepodong

S ummer vacation, the first since I'd enrolled at Korean school, came to an end. I went to school all during break, though, because I had practice. I was on the volleyball team, but I still had yet to play volleyball. The seventh graders went to practice but were only allowed to collect the balls the older girls hit.

Tokyo was terribly hot that summer. The news reported about the heat wave for days. The soccer team had a game on the last day of summer break, and although the whole school was called in to cheer them on, I didn't bother to go. Why should I have to cheer on a team that I didn't belong to?

On the first day of school, the news aired wall-to-wall coverage about North Korea launching a Taepodong missile the day before. The missile had reportedly flown over Japan before falling into the ocean. The words NORTH KOREA, in bold print, practically jumped off the front pages of the newspapers on display at the train station kiosks, along with the words GENERAL ASSOCIATION

OF KOREAN RESIDENTS OF JAPAN—more commonly known as Chongryon.

North Korea was under the regime of Kim Jong Il, whose downy tuft of hair, resembling that of a baby, danced playfully on top of his head. The smiling face of Kim Jong Il with his unprecedented hairstyle and the grim face of the Chongryon chairman were plastered all over the TV screens and front pages. I felt some relief in not seeing the words KOREAN SCHOOL written anywhere, at least that I could see.

That morning, all I wished was to reach Jujo Station—where my school was—without incident. If I could get to the station, I would be safe. On the platform and in the train car, the stares being directed at me in my chima jeogori were frigid, the air tense as though someone might shout or throw themselves at me at any moment.

I held my bag in my left arm and clutched the front of my jeogori with my right hand, my body damp with cold sweat. I held my gaze down so as not to make eye contact with anyone and put in the earphones plugged into my Walkman. The music stayed off, though. I kept my ears perked for any movements nearby and onboard announcements. Someone let out a cough, almost jolting my heart out of my chest.

Two more stops to school. As the train lurched to a halt, several passengers inside the packed train lost their balance and nearly fell over. Someone apologized under their breath. The doors opened. A violent wave surged between the passengers who wanted off and those who didn't. Swept up in the wave, the passengers wanting to stay on were pushed out of the train along with the rest and forced to stand outside the doors and wait to board the train again. Behind them was a whole other line of people waiting to get on.

The train left the station more packed than when it had arrived.

One more stop. Struggling to breathe, I tilted my head upward. I angled my face toward the AC vent and took a big breath. I was nauseous and light-headed from looking down. Beads of sweat rolled down my forehead to the tip of my nose. I couldn't tell whether it was a cold sweat or just sweat. I promised myself a bottle of water as soon as I got off. *Just get through this*, I thought, swallowing hard.

The train slowed into the station and stopped. The only thing on my mind was the bottle of water I was going to buy. As dazed as I was, I held my bag tightly against my chest and leaned my body toward the doors so as not to get caught in the wave. Someone clicked their tongue. I started to turn my head, but came to my senses in time to glue my eyes back on the doors. *Don't make eye contact with anyone.*

The doors flew open. As the first passengers spilled out of the doors, I braced myself to ride the wave out. Someone behind me yanked hard on my bag. My foot came down on someone's foot, and I let out a fearful yelp. I fell against the rush of people and was spun backwards where I stood. The earphones fell out of my ears. They got snagged between the crush of people and were pulled farther and farther away from me, dragging the

Walkman out of the outer pocket of my bag and onto the floor with a crash. I panicked, just barely managing to steady myself from falling down with it. Then the wave swept me off the train.

The Walkman had been given to me by my appa. I had pestered my overworked father for three days with an ad for a Walkman, and two weeks later, he'd surprised me with a brand-new Walkman after I'd all but given up. I had to get it back no matter what.

I jumped back on the train and spotted the fluorescent-pink Walkman almost immediately. I grabbed it off the floor and looked for my earphones, thinking they couldn't have gone very far. The passengers came rushing back onto the train. I had no choice but to give up on the earphones. I turned back around toward the doors to get off—but the crowd pushed me back further into the train, then the doors closed. I was horrified. It had all happened in a matter of seconds. It wasn't until Ikebukuro Station that I managed to get off.

Once I was safely on the platform, I sat on a bench and downed the bottle of water that I bought from a vending machine in one gulp. I squeezed my bag against my chest, hoping that it might hide as much of the chima jeogori as possible. Ikebukuro Station in the morning was teeming with people fast-walking in every direction. Normally, I might have put on the theme song to Godzilla on the Walkman and enjoyed the scene, but not today. Wiping away the sweat from my brow, I gazed at the ordinary scene of people coming and going for about forty minutes. When I realized how much time had passed, I decided it was time to move on. I got up from the bench and took the stairs down. I decided to go to the PARCO department store nearby. Any will I had to go to school was long gone. The desire to get out of the chima jeogori as quickly as possible was stronger than my wanting to get to Jujo Station.

I walked with my eyes trained on the ground a few steps ahead of me, so as not to make eye contact with anyone. Where was I? I'd felt safe here yesterday. Now, suddenly, I sensed danger at every turn. The street corner ahead terrified me. When nothing happened once I got there, I wanted to laugh at myself. *What was I expecting to be around the corner? Who was going to be there, and what were they going to do with me? Don't be stupid*, I muttered to myself. *You're freaking yourself out.*

First period would be ending about now. Apparently, on the days I was absent, classes were held in Korean.

Most of the teachers at the Korean school were very warm people. Sure, we had some abusive teachers and some creeps, but every school had a couple. Otherwise, the teachers at the Korean school were passionate educators, caring, at times, to a fault about their students. When people thought of education in the Korean schools, they wrongly assumed that it was all about North Korea, but not once did I hear the teachers mention the place. No one talked about North Korea. Apart from the uniforms and the school assemblies and activities, Korean schools weren't any different from Japanese schools.

That was why the portraits of the Great Leaders appeared to me as a part of the scenery one day and as foreign objects the next, and yet another day, as if they were whispering. *What's got you bothered? What are you looking at? What do you think is the mistake here? On what grounds?*

The day after the missile launch, the existence of those portraits kept creeping back into my head.

The Kim Family

I bought a dress at the first store I entered without trying it on and changed in the nearest restroom. Only then was I finally able to breathe. As I browsed the store, the shop attendant had appeared shocked to see me in my chima jeogori. She would have been suspicious at seeing a student in any uniform, this being a weekday morning, but that day, she'd looked at me as if I was a monster.

Since I couldn't go home until school got out, I wandered aimlessly around town. After a while, I got bored and went into a family restaurant, ordered a refillable drink, and opened up the newspaper I'd bought at the convenience store.

Plastered across the pages were pictures of Kim Jong Il, with his baby-soft hair, and of the Chongryon chairman, along with articles about the Taepodong missile.

The bigger concern for me was not the North Korean missile, but the portraits in the classroom.

The portraits were meant to be expressions of gratitude toward the Kim family, I had heard, a symbol honoring North Korea for providing funding so Zainichi Koreans remaining in Japan after WWII could work to preserve their culture and be educated.

On the first New Year's after it was decided I would go to a Korean school, there was a family gathering at a relative's house in Nara. It was on that occasion a drunk uncle told me this story:

After the war, the South Korean side refused to send aid to the Zainichi in Japan. It was likely that after a period of Japanese colonial rule, South Korea was in no shape to look after themselves and the Zainichi. That the Zainichi were seen as traitors in their homeland might have had something to do with it too. That was because most of the Zainichi came from a region that was now South Korea, and while many were forcibly brought to Japan during the colonial period, there were those who crossed the ocean to flee the Japanese army and those who came to Japan before the colonial era looking for jobs. As it turned out, my uncle explained, North Korea was the side in a position to lend a helping hand.

"Although I doubt lending a hand was all they were doing," he added, with a knowing smile.

Gradually, a rift took shape, dividing the Zainichi Korean population into two groups: the General Association of Korean Residents in Japan, or Chongryon, and the Korean Residents Union in Japan, or Mindan. And so, an invisible thirty-eighth parallel line was drawn in Japan too.

"Even though we had Japanese citizenship during the occupation, when the war ended, we were treated like foreigners and assigned *Chosen-seki* status. *Chosen* here doesn't mean *North Korean*, mind you, but *Korean domicile*, a status of a stateless people. But because the homeland was split in two, it also became possible for us to choose South Korean citizenship. The problem was none of us knew how to go about doing it, and the rumor was your kid had a smaller chance of having to serve in the military if you had *Chosen-seki* status. South Korean or *Chosen-seki*—it didn't matter either way, as long as you stayed in Japan. But wait—it later became impossible to travel overseas with *Chosen-seki* status. Did we want to travel abroad like we'd dreamed about or not—that was the choice we were faced with."

His eyes and cheeks tinged with red, my uncle said dreamily, "Hawaii. Do you understand, Jinhee? Ah, maybe not yet. Hawaii is wonderful!"

Why did so many Zainichi Koreans choose South Korean citizenship? Although it's doubtful the answer for everyone was that they wanted to be able to vacation in nearby Hawaii, the majority of Zainichi who didn't become naturalized Japanese have South Korean citizenship.

"Do you know why I chose Nara as my home?" my uncle asked, bringing his face closer to mine than necessary. His breath, smelling of sake and kimchi, stank. I pinched my nose and leaned away a bit.

"Because you like deer?" I guessed, recalling the deer in the park, which Nara was famous for.

"No, silly. Think, we're in Nara Prefecture. Nara, get it? Nara, Jinhee."

"Nara . . ."

"Yes, Nara. *Uri nara.*"

Uri nara was Korean for "our country." I tried to stifle a laugh, but it came out anyway.

"Hey, I'm not cracking a joke here. Ah, you'll understand soon enough, Jinhee. You will." With that, my uncle brought an empty glass to his lips. When he realized there was nothing left to pour down his throat, he gazed at the empty glass for a moment, then lit up a cigarette and stared wistfully at the curls of smoke floating upward.

After we returned to Tokyo, Umma and I paid a visit to the temple in the neighborhood. It was a family tradition to go and pray for a good new year. We ran into an acquaintance on the way, and after the usual greetings, Umma gestured for me to wait somewhere else. I played innocent and lingered about, turning my ears toward the conversation meant only for adults.

"He's come home to us." The woman burst out crying, caring nothing of who might be watching. "He was in the labor camps, I think. He hasn't said anything to me yet, but his teeth . . . all of his teeth are missing. He's lost so much weight, I didn't recognize him at first. We sent so much money. So much! As soon as the payments stopped, they had no use for him, so they sent him to the labor camps. I'm sure of it. The North Koreans play dirty, I tell you! Lord knows how much money we paid to negotiate his release. Thank goodness. Thank heavens for this miracle. Truly. People don't come back from the camps, I know."

Just who did she get back? I wondered later that night. How much money did she have to pay? In North Korea, if a miracle happened, you could trade someone's life for money. What a fabulous country North Korea was! I needed only to go to school to glimpse the portraits of the Kim family, who was responsible for building and ruling over such a beautiful country.

The mistake!

I found the mistake. Why couldn't I spot such an obvious mistake before? It was the portraits hanging in the classroom. All of the portraits hanging throughout the school were the mistakes.

Finally, I felt a haze lift from me. I got up from my seat to fill my cup with more melon soda. The restaurant was unexpectedly busy for a Tuesday. I checked my watch. Lunch hour. The restaurant was crowded with office workers and shop attendants working in the area. The only seventh grader ditching school, slurping a soda with a newspaper spread in front of her, was me.

The Devils in the Amusement Arcade

The sun was dipping to the west. Yes, it had to be the west.

I troubled over whether to go straight home or to meet up with Nina at Jujo Station to ask her opinion of the portraits.

I decided to go to Jujo.

Jujo was a direct train from Ikebukuro Station, no transfers. Since I couldn't be seen changing at Jujo, I went back to PARCO and changed into my chima jeogori in the restroom. I didn't want anyone from school to see me out of uniform. There would be senpai at Jujo Station too. If I didn't show up in my uniform, acting like my usual self, people would find out that I'd ditched, and I preferred to have everyone except Nina thinking that I'd been sick. I wasn't exactly fond of ditching school. I wasn't any kind of delinquent and preferred not be lumped together with them. I might've crouched outside the store and ate a convenience store burger or two, but I hadn't completely lost my moral character—or so I'd believed at the time.

After school, girls in Japanese-school uniforms roamed around the department store in packs. They chatted happily about how this or that was cute. I stopped in my tracks for a moment, fixing my eyes on the girls. I couldn't help but wonder: If I had stayed at the Japanese school, would I have been able to wear a *normal* uniform, hiding my ethnicity, and hang out safely with other girls my age, regardless of whether a North Korean missile was launched or, worse, fell on Japan somewhere?

Suddenly I recalled the amusement arcade on the basement floor of the department store and decided to check it out for old times' sake. I used to go there with my friends and play in the purikura booths when I was in elementary school. We loved taking goofy pictures in the booths and seeing them turned instantly into sheets of stickers. We showed off our photo-sticker albums to each other and to classmates. The number of purikura you took with someone indicated the closeness of the friend-ship. I used to take quite a few purikura with a girl who was known as the class boss. We were good friends. We were always getting into mischief together, always prac-ticing the moves to the latest songs to perform them in the halls. Everyone knew we were close, and the puri-kura were proof of that. What would've happened if I had stayed at that school?

Getting to the amusement arcade in the basement required exiting the department store first. I went out and reentered the building from the side entrance, then took the escalator down to where there was a huge window from which the purikura booths toward the back of the arcade were visible. Inside the booths, with the curtains drawn, were groups of school girls clowning around taking photos. Though only their legs stuck out from beneath the curtain, you could tell they were having fun, their knee-length skirts swaying back and forth. I grabbed my long chima skirt and lifted the hem a little. My knees weren't anywhere near visible.

I made my way around the amusement arcade. I felt like a tourist wandering about, curiously observing the locals of a foreign city. I felt lost. I didn't know which way to go. Was this really the right path? Did I make the wrong choice? How were my friends from the Japanese school doing? What was Iguchi doing now? I didn't know where I was anymore. I realized I was roaming the amusement arcade, half expecting my old friends to show up.

"What are you doing?" It was a man's voice behind me.

I turned to find three men in black suits standing there. They looked like they were in their forties. They were tall and well-built like martial artists.

I felt a chill run through me. Their faces were completely expressionless.

"You from Korean school?" one of the men asked. He looked me up and down, like he suspected me of hiding a weapon or something. It was clear he wasn't an office worker, nor did he appear to be a security guard. His skin was tanned a golden brown. His heavyset brows suggested a stern demeanor. I nodded fearfully. The man fixed his eyes on mine, as though he were trying to see into my heart. I slammed the doors to my heart and turned the locks.

"Come over here," the same man said.

Saying nothing, the other two took up the rear to keep me from getting away.

The first man led us out of the arcade and stopped just outside the entrance. We stood in an area kitty-corner from the descending escalators, where the people coming off the escalators had to pass.

"What are you doing?" the man asked.

I couldn't tell if he was merely asking, or if he was angry.

"Nothing."

"You alone?"

"Yes."

The man grinned in satisfaction, then eyed the inside of the amusement arcade, a suspicious look passing over his face. Meanwhile, the other two, the first man's henchmen I supposed, disappeared for a moment and came right back. After exchanging glances with the others, the first man reared his arm back.

He's going to hit me!

I closed my eyes, shielding my face with my hands. What came down was not a fist, but laughter, a laugh meant only to convey contempt.

"Did you think you were going to get hit?"

Slowly I brought myself out of cowering, cursing my reflexes for giving away my terror. The man's eyes were black marbles sunk deep in the depths of darkness. They hardly looked human.

Yes, I did think he was going to hit me. But I couldn't bring myself to nod.

"Relax. We're cops."

I raised my head in surprise. Cops?

"There's a teacher named Lee at your school."

"Lee? Yes, there is."

"Is that scumbag always acting so high-and-mighty?"

"High-and-mighty? No, Lee Sensei is nice."

"That scumbag? The one with the gut?"

"Gut?"

"Stop repeating everything I say!"

"Lee Sensei is a woman," I answered a little too quickly.

"A woman?" The man raised his voice, making me flinch again. "Nah, the Lee I'm talking about is a man. Which school are you from? I thought you were from Jujo."

"Yes, but I only know the teachers at the junior high. Maybe the teacher you're talking about is at the high school, but I can't be sure."

As soon as the words were out of my mouth, I found myself leaning a hand against the window to keep from falling over. *What happened?* My left cheek was hot as if a bee had stung it. My vision was out of focus.

Did he hit me?

Yes. He'd slapped me across the face. The rainbow lights of the arcade reflected off the window. I raised my head and straightened up.

"Don't play innocent with me." He prodded my head with a hand several times as if to suggest there was nothing inside.

I wasn't about to give in. I looked him straight in the eye and answered point-blank, "Really, I don't know."

I tried to keep my head from spinning. *Don't give in. Don't cry*, I kept telling myself. I was probably glaring. Although I didn't mean to, my eyes were shooting daggers. The man clicked his tongue.

Two girls about my age, both in school uniforms, came down the escalator. Their faces clouded over as soon as they caught sight of me. As the girls made to turn back, the suited men, who'd called themselves police officers, smiled faintly and cleared a path for the girls to pass. The girls bowed and continued into the cheerful, dancing lights. Once they put some distance between us, I heard their relieved voices mix with laughter. "Wow, that was scary. What was going on back there? Ooh, scary!"

I turned in their direction to find the girls staring at me like I was some criminal before flinching and looking away again. Apparently, it wasn't the men they had found scary, but me.

"We're in the way here. Hey—" The man gestured with his chin for me to follow him.

He circled behind the escalator, where the lights of the arcade could not reach and the shadows were deep. If I blended into the shadows and disappeared into a blind spot, I knew I would be in danger. Alarms went off inside my head. The moment my body began to tremble, the two henchmen shoved me from behind.

Saying nothing, I stiffened my body like a weight and planted my legs firmly on the ground. Surrounded by two burly men, I felt more helpless than a shivering, yipping Chihuahua. The men grabbed me by the arm and, before I knew it, dragged me into the dark shadows of the escalator.

"Well, it doesn't matter. I suppose Lee will drop dead sooner or later," the first man said.

I was made to stand in a corner where the darkness was deepest. I could barely make out the lights behind the men. I fixed an imploring gaze at the lights. At times the lights were blocked by the men's heads and wavered. *Don't hesitate. Please. Help me.* The lights continued to waver from behind the men's outlines.

"You Koreans are dirty things, aren't you?"

The first man grabbed my chin so that I was looking up at his face. Letting go of my chin, slowly he traced a line from my cheek to my lips with a finger. My skin crawled. Seeing my reaction seemed to please him, a ghastly smile crossing his face.

"You have pretty skin, but what about your soul?"

The man ran a finger down the side of my neck, toying with my fear, then grabbed hold of my throat and squeezed. He applied just enough pressure so that I could just manage to get a breath. His voice poured into my ear. "So what about it?"

I put both hands on his enormous hand and tried desperately to get free of its grip. But the man's hand was immoveable. I tried to take in some air, but my throat caught, letting out a thin wheeze instead. The tears that I'd been holding back rolled down my face. The wall against my back felt unnaturally cold. *Someone will come and save me*, I thought, hoping against hope, but the chill of the wall seemed to tear that dream to shreds. I tried to shout with all my might. But with his hand around my throat, I couldn't even manage that. The amusement arcade, despite being within shouting distance, seemed miles away. I couldn't hear the laughing voices of the school kids, or anything, anymore. Behind the men, the ceiling lights danced wildly. The first man was laughing. Colder than the wall at my back, the sound froze my spirit in an instant and crushed it to pieces.

He's going to kill me.

As much as I tried to tell myself that it couldn't happen, I wasn't able to escape my own imagination. *If I'm going to die—*

I summoned all my strength and rammed a knee into the man's ribs.

He clicked his tongue with a look of surprise and let out a short laugh.

I gnashed my teeth so hard they made an awful sound, like two pieces of iron rubbing together. A pathetic moan came out of my mouth. More tears welled up and rolled down the sides of my face. A bitter feeling washed over me. My knee must have only glanced his side. It didn't feel as though I'd made solid contact. Still, I glared hard at the man's marble-like eyes and let out in a barely audible voice, "I'll kill you."

It came out as soft as an ant's breath, but it came out nevertheless. My body stopped trembling. I braced myself for the worst. I wanted at least to redeem myself before I died. *Keep calm, Jinhee. You're about to die. Keep calm.*

"Now, you see. I knew that's what you Koreans are about. You're dirty down to your soul."

With one hand still squeezing my neck, the man, red-faced, violently grabbed my breast with the other. In my shock, I nearly choked on a big gasp of air and coughed. An intense pain ran through me. As his damp breath blew into my ear, all I could do was cry.

I can't beat him. There's no beating a man this rotten. I could barely make out the blur of the ceiling lights, but nothing more. My hands were still grabbing the man's hand around my throat, but they probably barely registered as touching. I was a doll that he could do with as he pleased. The man's hand reached between my legs and touched me down there. I started and let out a gasp. And then—

The man let go and, in the next instant, snatched my head like a basketball and threw me down. I went tumbling across the floor. I lay there, still, and sobbed silently.

The man fixed the collar of his suit and patted down his midriff like he'd gotten some dirt on his shirt. After straightening his necktie, he spat out, "Damn, now I'm all dirty."

The man clicked his tongue and walked away.

Letter from
North Korea 3

To Father's Family Far Away

Hello, my name is Jina. I am sure this will come as a surprise, but I am your father's daughter. Father was forced to marry as soon as he arrived in North Korea. That would make us half sisters. The last letter you received from him was quite a few years ago. I apologize deeply for writing you so late. Father passed away soon after he sent the letter. The truth is he was sick for a very long time. Unfortunately, we had no way of getting him to a hospital. That would have required traveling over several mountains, and Father didn't have the strength. Even if he did manage to get over the mountains and to the hospital, he wouldn't have been seen by a doctor or received any medicine for reasons I can't explain in this letter. I hope you understand. Mother and I held his hand right up to the moment he took his last breath. I was heartbroken to see him suffer so and to be so completely powerless to help him. Father was a very kind man. I loved him with all my heart. It was very painful when he died, and I became inconsolable with grief and anger. But when I thought about how he didn't have to suffer anymore, and thought only of that, I felt some relief. We built his grave near the house. You might be sad if you saw how small it is, but it was the best we could do. If you should ever come to North Korea, we would be glad to show you to his grave. If you have no place to stay, I hope you will stay at our home. Until then, please know that we will look after his grave.

Jina

The Secret

It was raining. I didn't have an umbrella, but that suited me fine. I felt like walking home in the rain anyway. The headlights reflecting off the wet road dazzled almost to the point of blinding. Getting run over wouldn't have been a bad way to go. But running into the road would have required jumping over the landscaping separating the sidewalk from the street. I didn't have that kind of strength left in me. My feet dragged as I walked. The sidewalk was pitch dark unless a car passed. I continued to walk by the light of the moon.

He must have known that I wouldn't tell anyone. That I wouldn't go to the police. He must have known from the start. If he had tried only to choke me, I might have gone to the police. But it wasn't. It wasn't only that. That was why I wasn't going to tell my family, my friends, or anyone, much less the police, now or ever. With my tears mixing with rain, I didn't have to hold it in anymore.

After the school contacted Umma about my absence, she had called the police and spent the entire day in a panic. When I finally got home, I went straight to my room without so much as an apology and threw off the chima jeogori. I changed into a baggy T-shirt and a pair of shorts, but I didn't feel at all better.

The chima jeogori was dirty, but that hardly mattered now, soaked as it was from the rain. Neither my face nor body had any big cuts or bruises. As long as I didn't say that I was in pain, I seemed more or less intact. The thought of touching my body frightened me. It wasn't that I was raped. *That's right.* It wasn't that my body was violated or battered to leave any bruises.

Then why do I hurt so bad?

I couldn't bear it anymore, and I cried out with everything I had. The earth could crack and the sky could split open, destroying the world and me along with it for all I cared. Zeus could throw lightning bolts and destroy Mount Fuji, Hallasan, and Paektu Mountain into dust. National borders were nothing but graffiti. Why did I have to suffer like this because of someone else's graffiti?

"Jinhee!" I heard Umma yell my name from the first floor.

She's coming.

I started pushing pieces of furniture in front of the door, huffing and puffing. Umma stood outside the door, trying to muscle her way into the room. I managed to push a bookshelf between me and the door and filled it with as many books as I could. There wasn't anything Umma could do to open the door herself.

"Jinhee, has something happened? Please, tell me," she said weakly. "Please," she said again.

I didn't answer.

"Did you hear? None of the kids wore their jeogori today. Only you."

I couldn't believe my ears.

"All the other kids wore their gym uniforms. The news about the missile was everywhere by yesterday afternoon, and the school decided that students should wear their gym uniforms to school starting today. So, when I couldn't find you, I thought something had happened to you." Umma pushed out a labored breath and sniffled.

Recalling every last detail of the nightmare that had befallen me that day, I began scratching my arms with my fingernails, trying to fight back the feelings of regret and despair swelling up inside. I hunched into a ball, my knees pulled up to my chest in front of the pile of furniture, and ran my nails up and down. The nails broke skin, digging up tiny flecks of it, and carved out grooves down the length of my arms. A thin scarlet river, as hot as magma, trickled down to my wrists. Another river formed, then another, and another.

"Do you want to go back?" Umma asked. When I didn't answer, she asked, "Do you want to go back to the Japanese school?"

I didn't answer. Through the deepening silence, Umma waited patiently for my reply. Despite the door separating us, I could sense my mother's determination. She wasn't going to leave until she had an answer.

"I can't go back," I answered.

"What do you mean? Why can't you?"

"I can't go back. That's all."

"Okay, listen. Please, just listen, okay? One of the girls

109

was spat on by a man on a bicycle near the school today. Did something like that happen to you, Jinhee?"

"No."

"Nothing happened?"

"No."

"Are you sure?"

I fell silent again.

"Then why were you shouting? You shouted because something happened, isn't that right?"

"I don't know."

"Please, Jinhee. Please talk to me."

"I said nothing happened! Leave me alone!"

I threw a book at the door. Umma let out a cry. I heard her sobbing on the other side of the door. My body felt like a weight pulling me into the ground. I wanted to be dragged straight into a coffin. I hated to hear anyone crying. To hell with it all. I clapped my hands over my ears and closed my heavy eyelids. I was tired. Drained. I wanted everything to disappear and go away. All I wanted was to be left alone. I wished I could go to sleep and never wake up.

A Revolutionary in Training

I stopped going to school. Appa started coming home early from work. At home, he made jokes and did his best to keep the mood light. He didn't ask what had happened or what I was thinking, just gave me space until I was ready to talk. As easy and agreeable as Appa's approach was, it didn't rub off on Umma. Whenever she thought I might be coming out of my shell even a little, she would try to pry me out. She might have been doing it for my sake, but it only motivated me to stay clear of her.

Maybe it was out of that frustration that Umma dumped all of her anger on the school. "Why didn't anyone contact me, you know my daughter doesn't understand Korean!" She screamed at whoever was on the other end of the phone.

Three weeks passed since I'd stopped going to school. I refused to take Nina's calls, refused to talk to anyone from school.

One morning, I woke up to the sound of tapping. I got up and glanced out the window to find a sparrow.

Wake up! Wake up, I said! It seemed to say, tapping its beak against the glass.

At first there was the one then, after a while, another landed on the windowsill and started tapping too, until the first sparrow flew off, leaving just one again. When I reached out to put a hand on the window, the little bird flew away and was gone.

I felt a strange loneliness come over me.

There were books and photo albums scattered about the room, half-finished bottles of juice, carelessly rearranged furniture, the desk scribbled over with curse words in permanent ink, the closet stuffed with piles of messy clothes, and poems like alien incantations littering the floor.

Taking in my surroundings from the bed, I realized that a hopelessly depressing air, one that could suck the life force out of a person, now filled the room.

At some point, time had stopped, and there wasn't any sign that things were getting better. Did the sparrow tap on the window to tell me so? I doubted it, but couldn't think of any other reason the sparrow had chosen to pay me a visit.

I waited for Umma to leave the house to pick up Appa at the train station, then called Nina's house. After the phone rang three or four times, Nina's umma answered.

Reluctantly, I told her my name and asked if Nina was home.

"Jinhee? Are you okay? Aren't you going to school? What happened?" The questions came one after another.

Although I barely knew Nina's umma, I assumed she

was out to make me the subject of gossip, which made me want to curse her out. Resisting the urge to slam down the phone, I chuckled like an idiot and answered, "I'm fine. I'll be back soon. Yes, I've been gone a while." Then I asked again politely, "Is Nina home?"

"Why, yes, hold on one second," she said in Korean, and put me on hold.

A familiar classical piece issued from the phone, causing me to hold the receiver away from my ear. I hated the classical music that played when you were on hold. Turning the majesty of the original work into a cutesy arrangement was blasphemy. To distract my irritation, I stared out the window, through the lace curtains, at the parking lot.

"Jinhee? Is this Jinhee?" Nina's voice was full. "Are you okay? Sorry. I'm so sorry."

"What for? Why are you apologizing?"

"I forgot to tell you to come to school in your gym uniform."

"What are you saying? That's not your fault. I was the one that decided not to go cheer on the soccer team, which was why I didn't hear the announcement."

Nina was silent.

"I'm sorry. Anyway, I'm fine. Thanks, Nina. Besides, all that stuff about the uniforms didn't have anything to do with why I've been absent. I was just taking a break."

"No way," said Nina dubiously.

"It's true."

"Then why have you been absent? Why haven't you been in school?"

"School? Right, so what's been going on at school lately?"

Nina thought about it for a second, then said she was switching to the cordless phone so we could talk in private and put me on hold. I had to listen to that hideous classical music a second time. Meanwhile, my gaze drifted out the window to the parking lot again.

"Hello?" Nina said and, without waiting for an answer, picked up where she'd left off. "So, you remember that stuff with the missile, right?"

The word *missile* came out of Nina's mouth like she'd said it many times before. Not in any kind of thoughtless way, but in a way that suggested missiles were a normal part of her day.

"Things got really interesting after that. Someone called the school and said they poisoned the tap water, so the school had to tape all the faucets shut. Plus, the school shut down all the vending machines, so we had to buy drinks at the convenience store or bring our own water bottles to the hakkyo. And we were allowed to go off school grounds during recess—you know, so the kids that forgot could go buy something to drink. There was a rumor going around that some of the boys in the other grades, too, took the tape off the faucets and tried drinking the water. They'd have to be some kind of stupid if they really did that. They're just out to prove who's toughest. Isn't that dumb?"

"What about now? Are the faucets still taped up?"

"Not anymore. The school checked everything out, and I guess it was all just a scare. I mean, it had to be.

Then the school got another call saying they were going to kidnap some female students and leave them hanging naked somewhere, but that turned out to be just a threat too. In the end, it didn't seem anyone was out to do anything. There was one girl who got spit on, though."

"Yeah, I heard about that."

"So, can I ask why you haven't been coming to school? Do you not want to talk about it?"

"Well, no . . . I don't mind at all. When I think about it now, it's really a tiny thing."

"What is it?"

"It was the day after the missile launch, and I got to thinking about the portraits."

"Portraits? Of who?"

"The portraits in the classroom, of Kim Il Sung and Kim Jong Il."

"Oh, those."

"Haven't you ever wondered about those portraits? Like felt anything?"

"Hmm. Not especially. They've always been there. They don't mean anything."

"I don't know, maybe they do."

"They don't."

"So then I can take them down, right?"

"You can't."

"Why not? If they don't mean anything, why can't I take them down?"

"Because you can't."

"Why? They must mean something then."

"Because that isn't something for us to decide. That's

for the higher-ups to decide. I don't even think it's something the people at school can decide. It probably has to be someone even higher up."

"Higher up, like Chongryon?"

"Something like that, yeah. Probably."

"Those people aren't even at school to see anything. What if I take down the portraits and nobody notices?"

"*Those people*, Jinhee? Don't be stupid. Of course, someone will notice! Is that why you've been absent all this time? Thinking about this?"

"Yeah." I lied.

"What, really? Unbelievable. You're always thinking too hard about everything. You should take life more easily. Whatever you think about those portraits, a powerless kid isn't going to be able to do anything about it. I'd like to see those portraits taken down, too, to be honest. They're just creepy. But it isn't something that a couple of girls like us can do anything about. It's pointless to even think about it."

"Something we can't do anything about . . . Do you really believe that?"

"Of course I do. Why would anyone even try? All you're going to do is get slapped down. Unless some kind of revolution happens, those portraits are staying where they are, got it?"

For several moments, I remained silent. I heard the rattle of the carport door, and peeked outside to find Umma backing the car into the usual spot.

"Are you listening, Jinhee?"

"Don't tell anyone, all right?"

"About what?"

"I'm actually a revolutionary in training."

"What are you saying? You're so stupid! Pabo!"

"Hey, I know what *pabo* means."

"So what? That's what I've been saying, *stupid*."

"I have to go. My umma's back."

"Okay. I'll wait for you at the train station tomorrow, okay?"

"What?"

"At the train station, tomorrow. You have to come to school, okay? It's boring without you there."

I didn't answer.

"Please, Jinhee? I'm sure there'll be some good news tomorrow."

"About what?"

"When you come, you'll find out."

I heard the sound of the front door open.

"All right, I'll see you tomorrow. I really do have to hang up. See you."

"Okay."

"And, oh, Nina? Thanks."

"Oh, no. Thanks for calling. I'll be waiting. Bye."

I hung up the phone right away.

My heart was pounding.

A revolutionary in training.

The words had an amazing ring to them. I thought about the idea of a revolution until it was time for dinner. Nina—a girl who'd attended Korean school since elementary school, who'd never gone to Japanese school—said she wanted to see the portraits taken down.

117

She said they were creepy, that they didn't mean anything. She was wrong. They did have meaning. A whole
lot of meaning. Maybe I could never understand exactly
what. But judging from the way the North Korean missile
had cast a huge shadow over the school, I knew exactly
the meaning the portraits would come to have.

In the end, nothing happened. It turned out to be
just a scare. An empty threat. *Don't make me laugh.* My
body trembled with anger. My body, which had felt like a
weight since that day, was itching to do something.

A revolution. As I repeated that word in my head, an
energy so hot that it might burn my body to ash surged
out of me. I felt as if I might explode at any moment,
on the verge of erupting with molten, hissing lava. I was
humming with joy.

She was back. The old Jinhee was back.

The Manifesto

It is time for us to rise! For ourselves and for future students!

If we do not organize to support those whose rights and lives are being trampled upon in North Korea, for those who risked their lives to escape it, and for the abductees around the world, any criticism against the Kim regime and against the Korean schools responsible for hanging their portraits will continue to be aimed at us, the students. We must make it known to the world that we do not stand with the Kim regime. Sooner or later, the Kim regime will surely crumble—it must crumble. When that day comes, students of Korean schools will suffer more criticism, more discrimination, and more violence than ever before. As the world raises its voice in celebration, our schools, which have worked to preserve the culture and arts of the Korean people, will be destroyed, and students will be made to live as sinners. Ask yourselves whether you can bear such a future. I, for one, cannot. The grown-ups are at the mercy of institutions. And so, it is up to us to take down every last portrait in the schools!

My fellow students attending Korean schools:

If you hear the word history *and feel that it is a story of the past, then you are gravely mistaken. We are making history as we speak. Indeed, Zainichi Koreans have been victims in the past. But the era of our victimhood ended long ago.*

North Korea launched a missile. However, the grown-ups declared it a "satellite." Whether it was a missile or a satellite, for us, the result has been the same. We have been threatened with poison and we have been spat on.

If we truly seek to protect our children, we must not be afraid of fighting for peace. This is also true of students. Doing exactly as the grown-ups tell us to do, we study our lessons with our heads bowed as if in worship of the portraits of two men who have no regard for life. "They've always been there." "They don't mean anything." "I've never supported them." "They have nothing to do with me." While these declarations may be true, as long as there exists the choice to boycott school, these are nothing more than excuses.

How many people in the world would believe such excuses? Those of us who live in Japan are in a position to fight back. We must not become people who live their lives influenced by others. We must not become people who are afraid of raising our voices and of acting. My fellow students, let us not turn away from this situation but meet it.

With this incident, the eyes of the world are on North Korea, now more than ever, and tensions are running high. No doubt criticism against the regime will increase. When that happens, the ones most vulnerable in Japan will be us—the children attending Korean schools. We must act now, before that happens. We must not fret, but think. We must imagine what it is that the rest of the world can see, but we students cannot. No doubt some of you are thinking, what will change by taking the portraits down? Let me be perfectly clear: There is a world of difference between having the portraits and not having them. This is only the first step. Let us rise together. It is time to take a hard look, not at the righteousness of others, but at our own!

The Last Fairy

Nina was waiting for me at Jujo Station as promised. She spotted me and waved her arms like we hadn't seen each other in decades. In her hand was a handkerchief, wrinkled from constant wringing. Without letting on how long she'd been waiting, Nina said "Morning," and smiled gently, perhaps to ease my nerves.

I'd been anxious since the night before. I questioned my sanity, even as I told Umma during dinner that I was going back to school. With a look of relief, Umma murmured, "I think it's time you went back too."

She washed my gym uniform, even though it was already clean, and began ironing my chima. We were supposed to go to school in our gym uniform and change into our chima jeogori in class.

"Did you put your books in your bag?" asked Umma as she ironed the pleats of the chima skirt with care.

"Yeah, I'm ready," I answered casually. The truth was my heart was pounding. *What if she looks inside my bag?* I was hiding hundreds of copies of my manifesto among my textbooks. I'd made copies at the convenience store.

As Nina and I started walking from the station to school, some of my classmates and senpai took notice. A couple of times, I turned around at the sound of my name to find a friend smiling and waving at me, always adding, "Welcome back."

The senpai, on the other hand, merely lowered their voices and whispered things to each other at the sight of me. I sped up and breezed right through them. I was trying to put up a brave front, of course—but despite my fear, it felt good.

Nothing had changed at the school. The security guard was standing at the front entrance and greeted students as usual. Minding the copies of the manifestos hidden in my bag, I said good morning with an innocent smile and shuffled off toward the shoe cubbies. Once I slipped on my indoor shoes, I felt like I was back in school.

Nina led me to a classroom on the second floor. All the girls from grades seven to nine were inside changing out of their gym uniforms into their chima jeogori.

Both layers of curtains were drawn, completely shutting out the sunlight. Classes weren't usually held there. The last time I was in the room was the time Ms. Ryang arranged the intervention between the high school girls and me after I'd gotten into trouble buying a cheese dog. It was that same dimly lit room, with several of the lightbulbs burnt out, in which the girls were now changing into their chima jeogori. I viewed the scene in amazement, like I was viewing it through a camera lens. All of the girls, including Nina, were changing as casually as you please. This upset me terribly. How could you joke and laugh like that, as if everything was all right?

Three weeks. In a matter of three weeks, this had become the norm. This was unacceptable. This could not stand as our *everyday*. We needed to wake up, understand, and think. The people threatening us were to blame. There was no mistaking that. But how did this happen? Why were we receiving threats in the first place? We had to confront this reality and think about it. Who was to blame? Why was this happening? What was at the core of all this?

"Hurry, Jinhee, or I'll have to go without you," Nina said, threading her slender arms through the white sleeves of her jeogori.

Nina belonged to the traditional Korean dance club. Having taken lessons since she was small, with the practiced hands of a dancer, she brought one end of the long blue sash over the other and tied it into a half bow at her left chest. The summer chima, which had lots of thin pleats, swayed elegantly above her ankles.

She gathered her hair into a neat bun on top of her head and tied it with a black hair band. In one fluid motion, she straightened the collar with both hands, then gently smoothed out the wrinkles in the sleeves. After checking the pleats on her skirt, she looked up with a satisfied smile.

Nina was beautiful. The chima jeogori looked perfect on her. Suddenly, I wanted to cry.

"Are you okay?" asked Nina.

"I just remembered."

"What?"

"I forgot my jeogori." I told another lie.

"Did you really?" said Nina in Korean.

"Yeah."

"It should be okay if you tell the teacher. Although, you'll stick out like a sore thumb in your gym clothes."

"That's okay. I would have stood out anyway in my jeogori."

Nina went with me to the teachers' room. As soon as they caught sight of me, the teachers let out a joyous gasp and welcomed me, all smiles. Ms. Ryang, who looked like she was about to cry, said, "Good to see you," in Korean and hugged me tight. I didn't hug her back.

While I was informing Ms. Ryang about forgetting my chima jeogori, the creepy math teacher said to me, "Never mind." Completely out of the blue.

I gave him a short "Okay." Then, teachers bombarded me with the same greetings one after the next, leaving me pretty tired.

After escaping the teachers' room, I went into the usual classroom only to be showered with the same greetings all over again.

"Jinhee! We've been worried about you."

"Sorry, thanks."

"Hey, where's your jeogori?"

"I forgot it."

"Oh, well, that's okay. No worries."

"Jinhee! Morning and welcome back! So, you're back at school."

"Yeah, morning."

"We were all so worried."

"Sorry, thanks."

"Hey, you know you can change into your jeogori upstairs."

"Yeah, I know. I forgot it."

"Oops."

"Hey, Jinhee? Jinhee's here! Annyeong, it's been a while."

"A while."

"Are you okay? Are you feeling all right?"

"I'm great. How are you?"

"Fine. We're all fine."

"Oh, that's good."

"Hey, you're still in your gym clothes?"

Yeah, I'm in my gym clothes; I'm great; I'm okay; Thanks for your thoughts.

All of the greetings had so worn me out that I barely remembered what happened during class. Only that every time the portraits caught my eye, I got into a staring match with the two Kims until my head throbbed. I didn't have anything on my desk except my arms. Since I'd supposedly returned from illness, no one dared to scold me. All of the teachers were very considerate and spoke to me encouragingly.

"I'll see you at the gym," Nina said, coming between me and the Kim family.

"The gym? What for?"

"Didn't I tell you there might be some good news?"

"What are we doing? Does that mean they're cutting class short?"

"Maybe by an hour."

"Hooray, I was falling asleep listening to the teacher's incantations."

"*Incantations*, Jinhee?" A crooked smile came across Nina's face.

I sat on the first floor of the gymnasium, three rows from the stage. Nina was nowhere in sight.

The red curtains on the stage were open, revealing two gigantic portraits of Kim Il Sung and Kim Jong Il. An old man with a microphone in one hand began to speak in Korean. The students and teachers burst into applause and seemed glad about something.

"Hyangeun! Hyangeun!" Turning around, I shouted at the girl sitting diagonally behind me.

"Shhh! What is it?"

"What is he saying?"

"We can go to school in our jeogori starting tomorrow."

"No. No way—"

"Hey, eyes forward. Nina's coming out."

When I turned back around, there were ten drums arranged in a straight line across the stage. Unlike Japanese taiko, these drums were the size of a frying pan suspended from a frame about two meters in height. Each drum was fixed at a height that the drummer could reach with bachi sticks.

A tense calm, like one before a storm, filled the gym, until Korean folk music came blaring out of the speakers. Dressed in an outfit that conjured up images of a wintry seascape, Nina spread her arms before her, fluttering the frills of the outfit like the wings of a fairy, and then began to dance as if floating on air.

Despite being surrounded by senpai, Nina was confident, poised. I trembled with emotion.

"Yangsoon!" someone shouted from the audience. One of the girls on stage smiled bashfully.

Ten girls with bachi sticks lined up in front of the drums, facing the audience. They struck the drums with their left hands once, twice, three times, in time with the folk music heard over the speakers. Then, as they kept a two-handed beat on the drums, the girls bent backwards and slowly turned once around where they stood. The ten girls were in complete sync. None of them missed a beat as they were turning. There was a huge applause. I clapped my hands until my palms hurt.

Nina was drumming on the third drum from the right with a big smile on her face. Not a fake smile, but one of pure happiness. She lowered herself into a crouch in front of the drum and rippled her arms like waves. The waves were small at first, then gradually grew bigger. While Nina danced in a squat, the girls on either side of her continued to drum standing, and the next girls squatted like Nina, their glittery blue sleeves moving like the fabric was alive. In this way, with the line split into five versus five, the girls alternately stood to play the drums or dance. They appeared to be battling one another. I swallowed hard, watching in anticipation of which side would emerge victorious.

"Nina!" shouted Jaehwan, standing two rows behind me. When his eyes found mine, he smiled.

I mouthed, *one, two*—

"Nina!" Jaehwan and I shouted together, and Nina's smile grew wider.

Nina continued to dance. She was so captivating in that gorgeous blue dress that I wondered whether she might have been born in it. Gradually, the alternating movements of the dancing and drumming came back in sync, until all of the girls spread their hands at the same height, leaped at the same speed, and struck the drums with the same intensity. Did they reconcile? Was the war over? Was peace restored?

Not a chance!

The portraits of the Kim family lurking behind Nina were laughing.

The music came to an end. The ten dancers, including Nina, bowed in unison and waved toward the seats, smiling with accomplishment. The gymnasium shook with thunderclaps of applause. Excitement filled every corner of the first and second floors.

Nina seemed to be looking for me. I waved at her, and noticing me right away, she beamed and waved back. When Nina and the enormous portraits came into the same line of sight, something Nina had said came back to me.

"You're always thinking too hard about everything, Jinhee." That was what Nina had said on the phone last night.

Thinking too hard. Maybe she was right.

"Whatever you think about those portraits, a powerless kid isn't going to be able to do anything about it."

A kid? Powerless? I wonder . . .

"I'd like to see those portraits taken down, too, to be honest. They're just creepy."

So, let's take them down. We'll take them down together.

"But it isn't something that a couple of kids like us can do anything about."

Kids, kids, kids . . . that's just an excuse.

"It's pointless to even think about it."

But what if the tap water really was poisoned and you drank it, Nina? Would it still be pointless to think about it?

"Why would anyone even try? All you're going to do is get smacked down."

I know exactly one person who would.

"Unless some kind of revolution happens, those portraits are staying where they are, got it?"

Okay, okay. I got it.

Standing on stage with the smiling portraits at her back, Nina waved at me one last time.

Me, Myself, and Nobody

After the performance, we were directed to go back to our classrooms. I raced out of the gymnasium ahead of everybody else and ran full tilt toward the middle-school building. The buildings at the Korean school were erected in gray concrete, like ruins.

I entered the building through the connecting passage and ran down the hall without bothering to change out of my outdoor shoes. All clear. Quiet. Not a security guard or teacher in sight. The sounds of my footsteps and breathing echoed in the halls. I bounded up the stairs, two steps at a time, without slowing my pace. The seventh-grade classrooms were on the top floor. I went around and around, up the stairwell to the second floor, the third floor, until finally I reached the fourth floor and bolted into the classroom.

Empty of people, the classroom looked like a sacred place. Half of the sun's rays coming in from the balcony were blocked out by the curtains, yet a soft light filled the room. It seemed everything had been orchestrated to make the classroom appear hallowed. The white dust floating in the air resembled tiny fairies. But the Kim family lingering over the blackboard spoiled the scene.

Just because you can rule North Korea doesn't mean you can rule Korean schools in Japan forever. If my dear friends ever get hurt because of the school's system or because of some grown-up's petty pride, I will destroy the school and show you what hell looks like!

I stopped at my desk, grabbed the copies of the manifesto out of my bag, and ran out into the hall. The sounds of countless footsteps coming up the stairs echoed from the stairwell, along with sounds of unrestrained laughter and rowdy yelling. I snatched a handful of the manifestos off the top of the stack and tossed them in the direction of the voices.

The papers fluttered in every direction. Some of them landed nearby, while others fell all the way down the length of the stairwell as intended. The papers took flight—*in search of change and freedom*, I thought. After I watched them go, I marched down the hall, throwing more papers up in the air. The papers scattered and dotted the floor, like patches on a calico cat.

"There's something on the floor," said a boy in Korean from the stairwell.

With the voice at my back, I went back inside the classroom and climbed on top of the teacher's desk. I held up the few remaining manifestos above my head, then sent them scattering to the floor. The last sheet fell and found its resting place in a pool of light filtering in through the trees.

Turning toward the blackboard, I reached for the

portraits. The frames hung on a string nailed on the wall, so they came down easily. Two rectangular imprints remained where the portraits used to be. I shuddered. The whiteness of the rectangles told how long the portraits had hung in the classroom.

"Jinhee, what are you doing?"

I turned. Jaehwan was looking up at me standing on the desk with the portraits in my hand, like I was a rabid dog that'd escaped from the animal hospital. *If only Jaehwan had suddenly appeared at the amusement arcade too*, I thought, almost in tears.

"Jinhee, calm down," Jaehwan said in a soothing voice, stepping slowly toward me so as not to provoke me. Behind him, my other classmates looked on stiffly.

"The arcade in Ikebukuro, the one in PARCO," I whispered.

"What?"

"Don't go."

With that, I swung my arms downward. Someone screamed. One of portraits caught the corner of the desk. The glass frame shattered, sending tiny shards of glass everywhere. At last, Kim Il Sung was revealed to be human. The smiling face whispered, *Did you solve the problem?* A crowd formed near the classroom door. They seemed to have forgotten how to breathe.

"What's all the commotion?"

It was the math teacher. There wasn't any time to lose.

"North Korea," I said in a full voice, "does not belong to the Kim regime. We are not students of murderers. The portraits will be removed right this moment. Take back the North Korean flag!" Before I knew it, the words rang out of me.

"Jinhee—"

As soon as the math teacher caught sight of me, he pushed the students aside and ran toward me with a look I'd never seen before. I jumped down from the teacher's desk and dashed for the balcony, when—

A terrible crash filled the room. Another missile? I snapped my head back to find someone's bag, textbooks, and pencil case scattered on the floor, after the math teacher's leg got caught on a hook on the side of a student desk where the bag had been hanging. Behind the math teacher, Ms. Ryang was also coming after me. I heaved open the sliding door to the balcony. The sliding glass door made a sound as if it might have shattered, but I didn't dare turn around. When I looked down below from the fourth floor, there wasn't a single soul outside. The students had all moved indoors.

Now was my chance. I reared back and, with all my might, threw the two portraits off the balcony. Before I could see them smash against the ground, before I could witness their total obliteration, the math teacher and Ms. Ryang grabbed me by the arms and dragged me back.

Inside, I couldn't bring myself to look at Jaehwan. I heard a girl sobbing. As the teachers dragged me out into the hall, I saw that the girl who was sobbing was Yunmi.

Why? was the word she seemed to mouth. Nina was nowhere in sight.

These Spaces

Whose job was it to distinguish *abnormal* from *normal?* Was it the job of gods? Or humans? I found myself in a state between abnormal and normal, waiting for my diagnosis.

I was in a space completely hidden from the outside world. But without question, it existed. Without the world out there, this space surely wouldn't exist. These spaces existed everywhere in society. Some people could claim to have spent time in more than a few of them, and those that have might say this:

"Life is just a bad joke."

Living a respectable life. Now who'd want to do something like that? He who laughed the most won. In the past, now and forever, he who laughed every day won at life. Life wasn't about big houses or expensive cars. If you had a gaping hole in your house, and you didn't have the guts to invite the wind in and let it get a whiff of what you were cooking, then you didn't interest me. All the self-pity and endless crying—I couldn't stand people like that.

Stamps

"Someone give me a cigarette," I said for some reason.

Maybe it was because the wallpaper looked as though it had been yellowed by cigarette smoke. The room was a nonsmoking room. The wallpaper was torn in places. It was also black with grime and stains. Thank God the stain didn't resemble anyone's face that I could recognize.

I got out of bed and sat on the table by the window. The window was bolted shut, so it was impossible to let fresh air into the room. I looked outside at the trees swaying in the wind and closed my eyes. As I imagined the breeze, I freed the loose strands of hair from behind my ears. The strands trickled down around my neck, giving me the illusion of a gentle wind.

There was nothing here, in this place. For me, that was a good thing. But there were many rules. You had to wake up at seven-thirty and have breakfast. If you were asleep, you were woken up. Lunch was at noon, dinner at six. The time between was always filled with something—the something depended on the day of the week. On Wednesdays, which happened to be my first day there, we did yoga stretches, and on Thursdays, a piano teacher came and led us in song. On Fridays, we had a general life meeting and Saturdays were a day off. On Sundays, we sang karaoke in the cafeteria, and on Mondays, we studied what we needed to go back to the outside world. On Tuesdays, we exercised on treadmills and other equipment.

Every time you participated, the doctor gave you a stamp. The more stamps the better. If you seriously wanted to leave the psychiatric ward, that is. If not, well, you didn't need any stamps at all.

Dear Harabeoji in Heaven

What if children were suffering before your eyes? What if by letting go of a little pride, grown-ups could solve a whole lot of problems? And what if in doing so, the future could be a little brighter for the children? Don't grown-ups owe it to their children to try? What if by giving voice to the discrimination and grievances of the world, we're turning a blind eye to the heart of the matter? What if in doing so, we're provoking a strengthening of nationalism? At lectures, while the Korean Peninsula's past is discussed, or whenever anyone discusses current issues, they always talk about them from the South Korean perspective. Let us discuss these things by skillfully considering the views of the South and North. As long as we are in North Korean school, shouldn't we discuss the North Korean problem thoroughly? Can you find a portrait of the South Korean president in the school? No. Not anywhere. Why go to North Korean school and turn a blind eye to North Korea as it is now? I was told that school and politics don't mix.

141

Then why do the portraits hang in the schools? "They are expressions of gratitude," *isn't any kind of reason. If anyone wants to be grateful, they're free to be grateful in their hearts. The portraits should be removed for the sake of the children. Grown-ups can be so unfair.*

To the Japanese people who threaten children, the schools refusing to change at the expense of children, and the stupid-ass murdering dictator—to hell with all of you. Harabeoji, I refuse to look away. I won't. I have blood relatives, ones I've never met, in North Korea. That's why, Harabeoji, I don't want to look away. Even if I make an enemy of everyone.

Harabeoji, please tell me one thing. Did you really mean it when you wrote that North Korea was a good place? You only wrote that because you'd be in danger when they read your letters, right? What did you really see? What were you feeling when you wrote those letters? I have hurt two people dear to you. I didn't grow up well at all. Aelin, your daughter. And her husband, my appa. All they ended up with is a broken family. They don't eat, and they look thinner every time they come to visit. They have the word tired *stamped on their backs. I robbed them of their smiles. What should I do, Harabeoji? Nina stopped coming to school. She refuses to talk to anyone. I didn't wish for that to happen. All I wanted was for girls to be able to go to school safely in their chima jeogori— that's what I wished for. If you're reading this in Heaven, please tell me. What did I do wrong? What should I do now? Just tell me, where is the enemy I should've been fighting? Who? Was I wrong? I have lost my name. I can no longer claim my Japanese name or my Korean name. At least, that's how I feel. Even when I want to fight, it feels like my resolve, like sparks over a flame, wavers and disappears. When I think not of the school, but of the people dear to me, I feel conflicted. Are North Korean schools really meant for the students risking their lives to go? Should the skeptics say nothing and walk away? What is worth the risk of going to school in the first place? The more I think about it, the more tangled and confused my brain gets. And so, I promise not to try anymore. That doesn't mean I'll forget, though. I haven't forgotten. If I am ever forgiven, maybe I'll see you and everyone in Heaven. Please forgive me for wishing it true.*

Jinhee

A Fragment of Time

Our history isn't some textbook that no one wants to open. Our history can be found in our music. The tears we shed can be found in our songs. Shrouded as our ancestors were in darkness, despite knowing their lives would likely end without notice, they never forgot to sing and dance and laugh. Their spirit is with us across time. As long as we, the inheritors of that spirit, give our lives to living, the music will never die. Our songs will continue to grow. Though a change may come, the day of our history's end will not. Do not fear. The world is filled with more art than textbooks.

Gummy Bears

As soon as I was back in my motel room, I grew wistful for the Oregon sky I'd just left behind, so I went outside again.

The motel, which cost twenty dollars a night, didn't have a heated pool or Jacuzzi. No restaurants or bars nearby, only a 7-Eleven about a fifteen-minute walk away. The lady behind the counter drinking a supersized Coke like it was water had turned off the lights at nine and gone home for the night. At check-in, I had to sign the agreement first, then pay the bill up-front. As long as she had those two things, the lady didn't seem to care what happened to the guests. At the time, there was a truck and two cars parked in the lot. Last night had been so quiet I could hardly sleep. It wasn't until morning that I finally nodded off.

Outside, the rain had let up. A cool breeze pinched my cheeks. Not a single cloud in the night sky. I spotted a plane in the distance. Sticking my legs through the railing of the second-floor walkway of the motel, I lowered myself onto the damp ground. I felt the moisture seeping into my jeans and recalled the open-air hall at school where I watched the shoes. I leaned forward, resting my head between the rails, and closed my eyes. I took in a deep breath and let myself forget who or where I was, if only for a bit. Swinging my legs back and forth made me feel as if I were floating on air, as if I could fly away to another planet.

"Hey, you sleeping?"

It was a man's voice. Slowly, I opened my heavy eyes to find a man with long hair standing next to the truck in the parking lot. He flashed a friendly smile and held up a small bag in his left hand.

"Do you want some gummy bears?"

"No thanks."

"You sure? Now, what am I gonna do? I can't eat anymore." He looked down at the bag for a moment, then up at me again. "I just want to give you these gummy bears. I'll give them to you, and then I'll go away."

After some hesitation, I nodded without smiling. The man bounded up the stairs on the left and came towards me. He sat down next to me, letting his legs dangle over the side of the railing like me, and dug his fingers into the tiny bag. He had the mannerisms of a kindergartner, but when I stole a look at his face, he looked at least ten years older than me.

"I have to tell you, I ate all the green gummies. Do you mind having the red ones?"

"No, I don't mind."

"Then, I guess that leaves me with the yellow ones."

"Are the green gummy bears your favorite?" I asked, chewing apart the red gummy in my mouth.

"Yep."

"The green ones are my favorite too."

"You see? I knew we'd get along. Do you want some more?" The man held out the bag.

I dug my fingers into the bag like he did. My fingers roamed over each gummy bear until they found a green one at the bottom of the bag.

"Lucky me!" I shouted, showing the man my discovery.

"Lucky you!" The man flashed a look of surprise, then smiled at me. When he laughed, his eyes squeezed into almost nothing. I looked ahead again and popped the green gummy bear into my mouth.

"Where are you headed?" the man asked.

"Where?"

"Aren't you on a trip or something?"

"Nope. I'm going home tomorrow."

"You have family here?"

"Not exactly. I'm in a homestay."

"Do you have to go home tomorrow?"

"It's what I promised."

"That's too bad. I was going to ask if you wanted to come with me."

"Come with you where?"

"San Diego. You know, in California?"

"I know San Diego. What for?"

"To go to the zoo."

"The zoo? You're driving for who knows how many days just to go to the zoo?"

"Yep. Always wanted to go there."

"But there has to be a zoo that's closer than San Diego."

"Well, the zoo in San Diego is special. All the others pale in comparison. Not that I've been there yet, but you can tell how special it is just by looking at the website."

"Why do you like animals?"

"That's easy. Because there isn't a bad one among 'em."

"No bad animals? I wonder . . . I mean, I've never talked to an animal before."

"Then let me ask you this. Do you think you could kill a rat?"

"A rat?"

"Uh-huh."

"Well, no."

"What about a bird?"

"No."

"What about a dog?"

"No, I said."

"What about a person?" he asked. "Could you kill another person?" the man asked again, fixing me with a direct look. I stared right back at him. I didn't want to say yes or no. Who knew what my face must have looked like then. The man muttered sorry and gave me a gentle pat on the head, like he was comforting an injured cat.

"Me too," he said in a whisper, then again, in an even lower voice. "Me too."

I closed my mouth, saying nothing.

"You can have the rest." The man held out the bag of gummy bears. I shook my head, but he set down the bag next to me and went on his way.

• • •

At eight the next morning, I closed the door behind me. The truck was still parked in the lot. The motel lady was behind the counter, eating a burger with a super-sized Coke. I slung the backpack over my shoulder, and gripping the notebook—which was now filled with fragments of memories that I'd jotted down over the past two days—I went up to the counter and handed back the key. With a sullen expression, the lady took the key from me and mumbled an empty "thank you" under her breath.

Another Star

"You can let me off here," I said to the taxi driver. We were driving on a mountain road in the middle of nowhere.

"You sure this is where you want to get off?" the driver asked, his face clouding.

"Yeah, I feel like walking a little."

The driver grunted indifferently. Including the tip, the fare came to thirty-five dollars. Since I hardly ever went out, I managed to save about fifty dollars a month, but the last couple of days had done some damage to my savings.

Stephanie's house was about a ten-minute walk away. Although it was raining, the sky in the distance was shining and beautiful. I grasped the notebook firmly in my hand. Although I was sure the memories would no longer escape me, I felt anxious without it.

As I approached the house, there was Stephanie at the window, looking at the sky. She was wrapped in a blanket, holding a mug in one hand. She must be drinking her favorite herbal tea. With a look at once adoring and worried, Stephanie held her gaze at the distant sky. Stopping just short of the front lawn, I stood in the road and watched her for a bit. Eventually Stephanie, bad eyes and all, noticed my lonely silhouette in the middle of the empty landscape.

As Stephanie disappeared from the window, I slowly made my way to the front door. The door flew open, and out came Stephanie, smiling like we hadn't seen each other in years. She wrapped me in a warm hug. Just then I remembered Nina—the way she had waited for me at Jujo Station.

"You're all wet," said Stephanie, slipping the blanket off her shoulders and draping it around mine.

"That's okay, I'm used to the Oregon rain."

"Well, you may be used to it, but your body certainly isn't. Let's go inside before you catch your death."

Stephanie wrapped her arms tightly around my shoulders and led me into the living room. I realized then the worry I'd caused her when I called her from the motel—the last two days too—and my heart ached.

Stephanie sat me down on a chair and lit a fire in the fireplace. Then she brought me a bath towel and tossed it over my head. Truly, she was like a mother to me.

"I'm going back to school," I said in my cheeriest voice. Once the words were out, a feeling of relief came over me as though I'd been set free of something.

"Oh, that isn't like you. Why?" Stephanie asked, matching my cheery voice.

"It's hard to explain."

"I won't understand unless you try."

"Well . . ." I sank into thought for a moment. "Can I tell you a weird story?"

"Sure. I love hearing weird stories." Stephanie smiled again.

"When I was in Japan, I took a trip to this really strange space. It was a real place, of course, but it was totally hidden from the rest of the world. While I was there, I used to gaze out at the stars from the window. And I met this tiny star. I tried talking to it and told her she was pretty. The star said to me, *I'm just a mass of garbage flying in space.* When I asked why she would say something like that, she answered that humans had told her so. I told the star that I had a similar name. She asked what it was, so I whispered so no one else could hear, *I've been called the human garbage of society. So, I guess that makes us both garbage.* After we had a short chuckle over that, I asked, *If the garbage in space could shine as brightly as you do, could garbage people like me shine someday?* At that, the star answered, *You will shine someday, I'm sure of it.* After a while, I became sleepy. I told the star that I'd see her tomorrow, but she said, *No, we can't.* She explained that the light I was seeing was from the distant past, and that tomorrow, she may no longer be shining. But then, she said, trying to reassure me, another star will always be shining tomorrow. Even if she's not the one shining, another star will always be shining, so it'll be all right."

"Ginny, what are you're trying to say?"

"I don't know. But maybe it's okay if I didn't try so hard all the time. If it's okay to take what life gives me,

I think I'd like that. Maybe I'm not meant to do anything. Maybe I'm meant to do nothing and just let life
happen. And it'll be all right, because another star will
always be shining. If I made like a shadow and disappeared, maybe that would put everyone's mind at ease.
But not a shadow that stands out. If I stand out, I'll be a
trouble to others again. Like getting expelled a second
time—"

"Ginny," Stephanie said softly.

Staring at the flame dancing in the fire place, I
recalled the lights in the amusement arcade.

"If you ever bump into that star again, be sure to let
her know there isn't anything at all special about seeing
stars shining."

"What?"

"Isn't that so? It doesn't do any good for any one
person to shine. The more lights the better, everyone
knows that. Would the world be better off if you settled
for being a shadow? Now, if you're going to tell me that
shadows are necessary to balance out the light—well,
honestly, Ginny, I don't want to talk to you. But you know
better, don't you?"

"I don't know . . ."

"Well, the star did get one thing right."

"Really?"

"Yes, that every person will surely shine. Everyone has
a moment when they will shine brighter than anyone.
You too, Ginny. That moment must come, and *you* have
to work at bringing it about. Not to become a shadow.
You mustn't run away. If you run, then it all ends there.

If you run once, it becomes habit, and you will run for the rest of your life."

"My past is always chasing me. It's a past I can't escape."

"You're right. You can't change the past. That's why you have to accept it, Ginny."

"Like the sky?"

"The sky?"

"It feels as if the sky is falling."

"The sky is falling. Ginny, what do you do?"

"I think I'd run inside a tunnel."

"And?"

"And it's dark . . ."

"Can you see anything?"

"Nothing. I can't see anything."

"Is anyone there?"

"No one."

"Ginny, what do you do?" Stephanie asked again.

I swallowed hard. My body went stiff. *Can I say it? Am I allowed to say it out loud?* Reading my worry, Stephanie smiled and gave me a slight nod. In an instant, the tension in my body left me.

"I would catch its fall."

As soon as the words were out, something inside me broke, letting out a flood of tears. I buried my face in the towel draped over my head and cried like a little kid.

Maybe I'd been waiting for the day someone would forgive me. I'd been waiting for the day someone would tell me that it was all right to forgive and accept the sky for the sky it was.

Stephanie drew me in and wrapped me in her arms.

As I leaned fully into her embrace, I felt as though I had reached the end of a long, seemingly endless journey and had come home at last.